CROSS-DRAW

'The Colt fell the short distance onto the worn carpet and Herne's body straightened up like a whiplash. But the hand that had dropped the gun didn't come back up empty. It had the hilt of the bayonet in it and midway through the movement the blade was unleashed across the room. Seth's mouth stayed open, words drained in mid-sentence; he moved the gun to fire but something plunged its way into his shoulder blade and pinned him to the door. His hand opened in spite of itself and the pistol slipped out . . .'

Also in this series

HERNE THE HUNTER 1: WHITE DEATH
HERNE THE HUNTER 2: RIVER OF BLOOD
HERNE THE HUNTER 3: THE BLACK WIDOW
HERNE THE HUNTER 4: SHADOW OF THE VULTURE
HERNE THE HUNTER 5: APACHE SQUAW
HERNE THE HUNTER 6: DEATH IN GOLD
HERNE THE HUNTER 7: DEATH RITES

and published by CORGI BOOKS

Herne the Hunter 8: Cross-Draw

John J. McLaglen

CORGI BOOKS
A DIVISION OF TRANSWORLD PUBLISHERS LTD

HERNE THE HUNTER 8:
CROSS -DRAW

A CORGI BOOK 0 552 10788 3

First publication in Great Britain

PRINTING HISTORY

Corgi edition published 1978

This book is set in Plantin 11/11½ pt. solid

Corgi Books are published by Transworld Publishers Ltd., Century House, 61–63 Uxbridge Road, Ealing, London, W5 5SA

Made and printed in Great Britain by Richard Clay (The Chaucer Press), Ltd., Bungay, Suffolk.

For Tony Albrecht:

everybody needs a friend these days
everybody rides their own damn ways

CHAPTER ONE

The man stepped through the opening at the front of the livery stable and looked across the street. Immediately opposite there was a single-storey building with the word 'Tonsorial' painted in black letters between window and roof. The large plate-glass window revealed a customer being shaved, the barber leaning over the chair, pausing every few seconds to wipe lather from the blade of the open razor onto the towel that hung over his left arm.

Further up the street there were a number of false-fronted stores advertising dry goods, groceries and liquors and the finest selection of boots and saddles in Wyoming Territory. The most impressive building in view was beyond these—The Cattlemen's House. It was a three-storey hotel made out of brick with two wooden balconies, one above the other, supported by thick wood pillars that rose up from the edge of the boardwalk. The ground floor contained a huge bar with a horseshoe-shaped counter at its centre and raised booths along three walls. Stairs at one corner led up to a first floor lobby and bedrooms on the floors above.

A group of cowboys rode noisily down the street, keeping their horses abreast, laughing and shouting at one another. They saw the man by the livery stable, saw him and ignored him. There didn't seem to be any reason why they should do any different.

The man watched them go by, looking at the pistols at

their belts, the low crown plainsman hats they mostly wore, the Double C brand that stood out clearly on the leather of their forty pound Denver saddles.

The rider at the near side of the line reined in his horse and called to the others. 'Gettin' me a shave. I'll see you at the Five Aces.'

He wheeled his mount round, pulling harder on the rein than was necessary; the animal tossed its head and whinnied and the cowboy slapped at its flanks with his open hand, making it rear up from the ground and swirl up dust.

'You aimin' to start a stampede all by yourself?'

The cowboy turned the horse again, staring down at the man who had spoken.

'That me you're talkin' to, mister?'

'Can't see no one else kickin' up dirt round here.'

'Well, you just mind your own damned business!'

The cowboy stared all the harder, the lines of his young mouth hardening into a sneer, the fingers of his right hand sliding back along his saddle until they were close to the pistol strapped down onto his leg.

The man watched him without moving, taking in the cowboy's gun hand and the changed expression on his face. 'Fer a man as earns his livin' in the saddle, you sure don't treat your horse with much respect.'

'What's that to you?'

'Never did like to see an animal treated bad. Sort of man who'd do that don't say much fer himself.' The man unbuttoned the single button of his worn leather coat with an easy movement. 'Don't take to gettin' my eyes full of dust, neither.'

The cowboy's fingers were resting on the leather of his holster now, stroking it. His eyes were narrow and the line of his mouth tighter than ever.

'I ain't gonna sit here an' be talked to like that. Not by no old man like you.'

'That so?'

The right flap of the coat moved back slowly. The butt of the Colt .45 was smooth with use; the thong at the bottom of the dull leather holster was tied inside the thigh. Without taking his eyes from the cowboy, the man used his thumb to flip back the smaller thong from the hammer.

'That so?' he repeated softly, talking almost to himself.

But the cowboy heard him well enough; heard him and saw the gun and looked at the stranger afresh. Couple of inches over six foot, long black hair that was greying at the temples, close to two hundred pounds. A face that was lined and weather-beaten; a hand that was veined and calloused hovering close to the Colt.

Somewhere in the back of the young cowboy's mind a warning clicked uneasily into place. He wasn't sure, couldn't be certain, but...

'You got anythin' more to say?'

The cowboy's hand shifted away from his holster and picked up the rein. 'No. Not fer now.'

'Best get that shave, then. There's a chair empty right by the window. No sense in waitin' around.'

The cowboy pulled his hat down firmly on his head and moved his horse slowly round. Without looking back he crossed the street and dismounted, tying the animal to the rail. He glanced up at the sign over the barber shop and walked in through the open doorway.

'Mister.'

The man turned fast, faster than you would have thought just watching him stand there seconds before. His hand was tight about the butt of the Colt and his body had dropped into the alert crouch of a trained gunfighter.

'Hey, steady now, mister! I didn't mean nothin'.'

The old timer from the livery stable had jumped back

towards the door, one hand raised and open, fingers shaking. They stayed that way until he saw that the man had gone back to his normal stance and let go of his gun.

'Just wanted to ask 'bout that chestnut you brung in, that's all.' He licked nervously with his tongue at the stained ends of his moustache.

'What about it?'

'Didn't say how long you was leavin' him.'

'That's cause I don't know.'

'Yeh, well, that's ... that's ...' He broke off talking and scratched the wisps of white hair that scattered his scalp.

'That's all right, then. Ain't it?'

'Guess so. Yep, sure is. That's fine.'

The man started to turn away.

'Mister.'

'Say your piece,' replied the man impatiently.

'That feller over there,' he pointed in the direction of the barber shop. 'Seemed like you was proddin' him awful hard to draw on you.'

'Could read it that way, I guess.'

'You know him or somethin'?'

'No.'

'Weren't sent into town to pick a fight with one of the Double C boys, by any chance?'

The man shifted his head to an angle for a moment. 'That likely?'

The old timer shrugged and scratched at his scalp again. 'You know what these big spreads are like—one always tryin' to cut the other down to size.'

'I heard of it happenin'. But no one paid me to do no cuttin'. Not this day, they ain't.'

'Then, mister, I'd say you're either plumb careless about your own life or you're itchin' fer a fight to let somethin' out of you that's crawled right up agin' your spine.'

The man turned his head aside and spat down into the

dirt of the street. 'You always so free with what you think?'

The old man grinned: 'When I can get someone as'll listen.'

'Tell you what, try talkin' to some of them horses you got shut up in there. That way there's no chance of them walkin' out on you.'

And the man stepped away and began to cross the street towards The Cattlemen's House. The old timer watched him go, observing the walk of a man who wasn't about to step aside for anyone, who likely never had—not since the day he'd first strapped that Colt .45 to his side. He pulled at a strand of white hair and pushed his tongue up into the yellow and brown hairs in the middle of his otherwise white moustache, sure that he'd seen the man before but unable to remember where.

It could have been back in '59 when the Pony Express was pushing westwards from Fort Bridger, beating the snows of the Sierras and the marauding attacks of the Paiutes.

It could have been during the Civil War, when Captain William Clarke Quantrill and his bloody guerillas were raiding deep into enemy territory.

It could have been in the South-West in the early sixties, playing fast and loose with Geronimo's Apaches among spirals of red rock that burnt at a touch.

It could have been in '78 fighting in the Lincoln County Range War, alongside of Billy Bonney and Pat Garrett.

Could have been earlier in that spring of '84, standing by the graves of the two young women he'd loved. Loved and buried them both, then stood by the mounds of earth without a tear to cry. Instead he held a bitterness tight inside him, venomous like the poison of the snake the old timer had reckoned he had curled round his spine. Ready to strike.

His name was Jedediah Travis Herne: the man they called Herne the Hunter.

Jed Herne edged his way between two cattle dealers and flipped a silver piece onto the polished surface of the bar. When the barkeep had sidled down towards him, Herne ordered a bottle of bourbon and a glass.

The barkeep squinted up at Herne and reached beneath the counter for a bottle of Jim Beam. He set it down and made good and sure that the glass he put next to it was clean and unchipped.

'Thanks, mister.' He dropped the change into Herne's left hand. 'You new in town?'

Herne dropped the coins into his coat pocket and picked up bottle and glass without a word. He headed for a booth at the furthest end of the room, seeking a position from which he could see the door and where it was impossible for anyone to sneak up on him from behind. Ever since what had happened to Wild Bill . . .

Besides, Herne had things on his mind and he wanted to be alone with them. Alone with a bottle so's he could drink them away.

The cowboy's name was Tolly Richman and by the time he'd got himself sat in the first chair of Eli Pullum's fancily-named barber shop his mood had changed from bad to worse.

He fidgeted under the striped blue and white cloth that Eli tucked up to his neck and scowled. 'This your place?'

'Surely is,' said Eli with a quick smile. 'Every brick of it.'

'Looks like timber to me.'

'Well,' said Eli, whisking up lather in a shaving mug, 'you're right of course. Boards like most others in town. Brick was just a manner of speech, you might say.'

'Like that fancy sign you got painted up outside?'

'Quite so. If you'll just let your head fall back like ...'

Tolly twisted his head to one side and took a cloud of white lather on the chin. 'What's it mean anyhow?'

'Tonsorial? Tonsorial refers to the work of a barber, sir. From the rite of shaving the crown of the heads of monks in Europe.'

'Huh!' He was none the wiser.

Eli settled his customer's head back in the chair and began soaping underneath his chin. 'To tell you the truth, sir, since you are so interested, the sign should have read tonsorial parlour. Trouble was, the signwriter I hired was too ambitious. Painted the first word so high there wasn't room for the second.' He lathered under Tolly's nose. 'Did himself out of half his money, though. Payment by the word, you know, sir. Payment by the word. Did I ... ?'

'Damn it!' said Tolly angrily. 'Why is it that every blasted barber I come across can't shut his mouth for more than a second at a time? Stop blatherin' on and get me shaved. I got friends to meet and some drinkin' to get done.' He stared hard at the barber. 'That clear?'

Eli nodded and set down the brush and mug.

'Abundantly, sir.'

Eli moved Tolly's head to one side and slid the razor along his left cheek, lifting away both lather and the first layer of beard. Then he turned his wrist and slanted the razor back in the opposite direction.

Tolly closed his eyes; the barber began to whistle. He shaved the other cheek and set the cowboy's head back so that his face was pointing at the ceiling. With forefinger and thumb he raised the tip of Tolly's nose and eased the blade of his razor underneath the bridge.

He was still whistling. Tolly was thinking about the big man he'd backed down from in the street; remembering it and not liking it one little bit. He started to scowl and Eli, sensing the contours of his customer's face about to twitch, increased slightly the pressure he was applying to Tolly's nose.

Tolly jerked back suddenly: 'Stop that blasted whistlin'!' And as he opened his mouth to speak the razor slid through his upper lip as easy as a knife through a piece of rarest steak.

Tolly yelled and flung up an arm, pushing the barber back across the room. There was a clatter as mugs and brushes fell to the floor and then Eli was picking himself up while the cowboy jumped out of the chair and moved closer to the mirror.

The white lather about his mouth was rapidly changing to a deep shade of red. Tolly lifted up the striped cloth and wiped the lather clear. Stared. More than three inches of upper lip were hanging forward like a sagging envelope and blood was flowing easily over the pink edge of flesh and dribbling down both sides of his mouth and onto his chin and neck.

Tolly continued to stare at the mirror for seconds that seemed to Eli like minutes. Slowly, as silently as he could, the barber began to move backwards in the direction of the shop door. Moving on hands and knees, his eyes never leaving the reflection of the bleeding face in the mirror.

He got to within three feet of the doorway.

Tolly whirled round and with his left hand he tore at the white tape that held the apron in a bow at the back. 'You damn butcher! You dumb bastard! You cut me! You cut me bad!'

He lifted his left hand to his face and pushed at the flap of lip. It pressed a bubble of pink air out into the barber shop and both men watch it fascinated as it plopped slowly onto the back of the barber's chair and burst.

Eli involuntarily drew breath and Tolly's right hand dived for his gun. Eli jumped backwards for where he thought the opening was and felt his back slam against the wall. There was a loud explosion that seemed to fill the shop with sound, a flash of deep orange flame and Eli's body was thrown back against the wall a second time, a strangled cry emerging from his mouth.

Tolly reached for the chair and hurled it across the room. The pistol was still in his hand and his eyes were tight and narrow. Eli looked at the left side of his white shirt where the material had been torn away and pumped into the gap between his ribs. He pressed his fingers to the wound and closed his eyes with terror as the tips sank softly inside.

'Bastard! Butcherin' bastard!'

Hands hauled him up and something hit him and kept hitting him and Eli didn't know what it was; eyes firmly shut and extremes of pain screaming inside brain and body.

Tolly threw the barber back against the side wall and lashed out at him with the barrel of his gun. Eli was full stretch on the boards and starting to crawl along them, a little moaning noise coming from between his lips. A trail of thin blood meandered over the floor like the track of a snail.

'N . . . n . . . n . . .'

Tolly bent down and lifted the barber up by his neck and arm; he spun him round and took a step away; then another.

The pistol came up and Tolly squinted along the barrel. For the first time in minutes, Eli opened his eyes.

'Nooo!'

His hands reached forward, begging, praying.

Tolly squeezed gently back on the trigger.

The barber's body was hammered backwards, his feet lifted off the floor. Arms flung wide, eyes bulging, he crashed through the middle of the plate glass window and landed with a thump on the boardwalk outside.

Tolly heard a woman's high-pitched scream and men's raised voices and started to run. He was out of the door and a third of the way across the street, heading for the saloon where his friends were waiting when a shot rang out.

He turned fast and saw a man coming towards him, walking slow, a rifle held in both hands, lawman's badge clear on his shirt.

'Hold it, son, or the next one'll be aimed fer you.'

The lawman was wrong. The next shot was Tolly's and it took the deputy in the neck and severed the artery. The rifle curved up into the air and the man fell backwards, already losing blood heavily from his wound.

By the time Tolly had got inside the saloon, the deputy was in the middle of the street, dead, blood continuing to spurt from his neck, mingling with the dirt and dust of its uneven surface.

CHAPTER TWO

From his booth at the back of The Cattlemen's House, Herne heard both shots, the second more distinctly than the first. He shifted in his seat, straightening his back, touching the butt of his Colt lightly with the palm of his right hand, as if for luck. Then he took the bottle and poured himself another drink. Whatever was going on out in the street, it wasn't his concern.

He grinned briefly at his reflection in the side of the glass. Down by the livery stable, he'd done something he hadn't done in a coon's age—almost prodded some feller he didn't know into going for his gun. And without any reason other than feeling like a little action.

Herne set the glass to his lips and drank.

Maybe the old timer had been right. What was it? Something about poison wanting to get out of his body. Well, if he did feel like that he had good reasons. His wife, Louise, attacked and raped by a gang of drunken gamblers and her mind so affected by it that she had taken her own life. Becky choking on her own blood in a hotel room with nothing he could do but watch her die. Friends like . . .

Friends like . . .

Damn it! Seemed like every friend he'd ever had had gone. Dry-gulched in some aroyo out in the middle of nowhere. Shot in the back in the dark of an alley. Gunned down by some young punk kid the day those twinges in the arm made the action that second too slow.

Herne thought about the albino, Whitey Coburn,

spilling his life out over pieces of gold he'd never own in the fetid squalor of a New Orleans warehouse.

It didn't seem to Herne, as he finished his shot of bourbon, that he had a friend left anywhere. It was just him now. A gunfighter fast approaching the wrong side of forty. His time running out.

One thing was certain—more certain than ever before—incidents like that back there by the livery stable, there'd be no more of those. He couldn't afford to do time's work for it. Throwing his life into the balance for no reward.

More shots sounded from down the street. Herne tipped the neck of the bottle one more time.

Tolly Richman had made it to The Five Aces saloon. He hadn't even stopped long enough to be certain what had happened to the lawman he'd shot. Tolly had carried on across the street as fast as he could, finally pushing through the bat-wing doors and skidding to a halt by the first of the tables. The pistol was still clasped tight in his right hand.

'Damn, Tolly! We guessed it was you causin' all that ruckus.'

'Would've come to see if you needed any help, 'cept we was busy drinkin'.'

The boys from the Double C laughed and banged bottles and glasses on the bar. Tolly stared at them through narrowed eyes, not moving.

'Shay. Get to the door.'

The big cowboy at the end of the line shifted so that his back rested against the counter. 'You expectin' company, Tolly?'

'Do what I damn well say!'

Shay looked at the others. 'Hear that? Put a gun in his hand an' he thinks he's ramroddin' the outfit.' The big man stood up and stepped away from the bar. 'Well that ain't the way I say it goes.'

Tolly jerked his head towards the door. 'Way you say ain't likely goin' t' matter much. There's some lawman out there in the street.'

'What's he doing there, Tolly?' asked Paulie Yates.

'I shot him.'

The cowboys looked at Tolly in silence. Then one of them whistled and another said softly: 'Sweet damnation.'

'Paulie, you take a look,' said Shay. 'But be careful.'

They waited while the cowboy moved to the doors. He was shorter than the rest, hat hanging down behind his head, stocky, bandy legs. He squinted down the street and turned back into the saloon.

'He ain't kiddin'. There's folks startin' to lift him away and they ain't handlin' him like he's more than dead.'

'Jesus!' said Shay, banging his open hand down onto the counter of the bar. 'So you finally did it, Tolly. You finally shot yourself a marshal.'

Tolly sneered, half in pride, half in fear. He slid the gun back into his holster and went up to the bar to pour himself a drink. The Double C boys made room for him and the bartender, sweating more than a little, watched him carefully from the far end of the counter.

There were only four others in the saloon; a couple of old men who'd forgotten all about their unfinished glasses of beer; a youngster who hadn't properly come round from the previous night's drunk and a gambler who had been hoping to pick up some of the cowboy's wages before they drifted off out of town. He sat there and shuffled his pack of cards, calculating the odds of them letting him simply get up and walk out of there.

They didn't seem to be very good.

'What you do it for, Tolly? Why d'you kill him?'

'He was comin' fer me. Took a shot at me.'

'Why'd he do that?'

Tolly grinned: 'Maybe cause of what I did to the town barber.'

'What was that, Tolly?'

Tolly's grin grew into an open laugh. 'Killed him.'

'Jesus!' said Shay. 'Holy Jesus Christ!'

'Quit beefin', Shay,' said Tolly. 'It ain't your trouble.'

The big cowboy rounded on him, anger showing in his large blue eyes. 'Like all hell it ain't. What you think they're goin' t' do? Let us ride out of here like nothing happened?'

'I told you, Shay, it ain't your fight!' Tolly's eyes had narrowed again; the line of his mouth was like a pencil mark below the clotted blood that clung to his upper lip. Here and there white splotches of lather hung beneath his chin and on one side of his face. His right hand hovered over his holster.

Shay backed several paces away, making room for himself to get his own pistol into action.

At the end of the bar, the barkeep thought about the sawed-off shotgun that was hanging on a couple of nails under the counter. The gambler had stopped shuffling the pack and was turning the cards over, face upwards, one at a time; not looking at them. The old timers still stared, still forgot their beer. The kid reckoned it was likely a dream.

The rest of the Double C cowboys watched also, unable to work out what to do or what they wanted to happen.

Then Paulie Yates took a pace towards Shay. 'Ain't no sense in it, Shay. No good fightin' among ourselves. We got enough on our hands gettin' out of here. Need every gun we got.'

'He's right, Shay,' said one of the others. 'No sense you and Tolly facin' off that way. Let's get us out of here.'

Tolly let his hand move an inch away from his gun butt and Shay did the same.

'Why don't you let me make a run fer it on my own?' Tolly tried again.

'Cause you already come runnin' here.'

'Cause you're Double C same as us,' said Paulie. 'An'

when chips are down that's what counts.'

'All right.' Shay pointed at one of the cowboys. 'Go check our horses are still outside. Tolly, where's yours?'

Tolly shrugged. 'Up by the barber's, I guess.'

Shay made a face. The cowboy peered through the batwing doors.

'They're still here, Shay.'

'How's it look? What's happenin' out in the street?'

'Nothin'. Nobody in sight either way. Like the place's gone to sleep.'

'Right. Now take it easy and see if you can get to one of the horses. Paulie, you cover him. If you can mount up, head over for Tolly's horse and ride it back here. We'll be waitin'.'

The cowboy looked at Shay anxiously, but there was no way of backing down. He pushed one of the doors gently back and stepped out onto the boardwalk. Looked around and stepped towards the hitching post where the animals were tethered.

Behind him, Paulie levelled his Colt between the batwing doors and watched. Waited.

There were two shots, almost simultaneously, from across the street. Neither of them was accurate. The rifle shells ricocheted off the front of the Five Aces. The Double C cowboy lay flat on the boardwalk, one arm over his head.

'Get back!' yelled Paulie Yates and triggered off a shot at the windows opposite. Tolly had ducked down by the side of the door, his own pistol drawn and ready. Shay and one of the other cowboys were close by the saloon window.

The Double C man crawled back inside, just as a volley of shots sang out from the far side of the street. Tolly and Paulie Yates answered quickly and Shay smashed a pane from the saloon window with the barrel of his pistol and started shooting in the direction of the puffs of rifle smoke.

And now someone else was joining in from further up

the street.

'Ain't there no back way out of here?'

'Wouldn't be much use. Not with the horses out front. We sure ain't about to walk away from no posse.'

'What the hell folk in this town want to carry on like this for anyways?'

'Right. Why don't they mind their own damned business?'

'Maybe they figure gettin' one of their lawmen gunned down for no good reason is their business.' The bartender had got to within a foot of the shot gun. He was sweating a deal more now and, out of sight, his hands shook a little.

Tolly turned his head and told the man to keep his mouth shut, then hastily snapped off a shot across the street.

'What d'you think?'

'I think we make a run fer it.'

Shay stood up and holstered his gun. 'Tolly, you ride double with Charlie. Paulie an' me'll cover the rest of you till you're mounted up. Then you do the same for us.'

'But . . .'

'No buts. That's what we're doin'. An' now. So move it.'

The cowboys readied themselves, Shay taking the window and Paulie Yates the door. Behind them the barkeep eyed the gambler who had stopped laying out the cards. The two men nodded to each other and the gambler rested his right arm on the edge of the table. One sharp movement and the pressure would release the small deringer he kept on a spring-loaded clip inside his sleeve. That would close up the odds more than a little.

Shay and Paulie began firing at the same moment; the four Double C men went through the bat-wing doors at a crouch, scrambling towards their horses. Charlie hauled himself up into the saddle first. As his right leg was swinging down into the stirrup, a .44 slug took him high in the shoulder, whirling him about and back down towards the ground. One of the other cowboys yelled with surprise as a shell stroked a straight line down his hand and forearm.

Tolly dropped into a kneeling position and took aim; there were three men running towards them from higher up the street, supported by a flurry of fire from a variety of weapons. Tolly took a bead on the leading man and dropped him with a single shot. His second missed its target; the third wounded one of the oncomers in the leg.

'Get back inside!' Shay's voice boomed out through the roar of gunfire and the cowboys bolted for the saloon door. All except Charlie.

His horse was galloping the length of the street, spooked by the heavy shooting. Charlie's boot had got jammed in the stirrup and he was being dragged with it, head and shoulders bouncing from the uneven ground. Charlie was only part conscious, vainly trying to reach down to his leg.

As the stampeding horse rushed past them, several of the good citizens of Liberation emptied the chambers of their guns into Charlie's body. It was good target practice and kind of fun to watch the cowboy's form buck and leap as it sped through the dust.

'Jesus! See what them mad bastards are doin' to Charlie?'

'Sweet damn!'

Tolly wiped at his forehead with his right arm and as he did so, he saw underneath the edge of his shirt sleeve the movement behind the bar.

'Look out!'

He had a long way to go for his gun and besides he was ducking away to the left fast, seeing the barrels of the American Arms 12-gauge shotgun poking over the counter of the bar.

Paulie Yates spun round, too, but slower than Tolly. He took the full force of both barrels from less than twenty feet. The blast picked him up and hurled him towards the wall like he was a bundle of rags.

Tolly fired at the barkeep, missed, bent low and ran

for the end of the bar. Shay was down behind an upturned table, pushing his pistol round its side. The others were torn between covering the street and watching their backs. One of the old timers made the mistake of moving too suddenly and nearly got his head blown off; instead he saw his beer glass smashed to smithereens in front of him.

The barkeep hurled the shotgun at Tolly and made a leap for the top of the counter. He was straddling it, staring across at the gambler for help that he must have known wasn't going to come, when the cowboy's first shot ripped into his right buttock. The impact sent him down to the end of the bar, arms thrown sideways part in an attempt to keep balance, part reaction to the wound.

He was reaching round towards it when Tolly's second bullet smacked into the base of his spine. The arm stopped moving; the fingers opened out into a curve then froze. His head came back as if pulled by an invisible wire and his body arched further backwards. Tolly saw the face upside down, the mouth open wide, tongue and teeth and the beginnings of a torrent of blood.

He fired a third time: the barkeep's face exploded before his eyes.

'Tolly!'

Tolly looked round quickly, responding to Shay's call. The gambler had dived to the floor and was trying to burrow under the chairs; the two old men had scuttled into the far corner behind the upright piano; most of the Double C boys were engaged with what was going on out in the street.

There was a skylight two-thirds of the way back and Tolly saw that it had been prised open. The barrel of a rifle appeared through the dark space and a shot went crashing into the table Shay was using as a shield.

Tolly ducked down alongside the bar and fired for the gap. Nothing. The rifle fired again and both Shay and Tolly replied. And again.

'Damn it!'

Shay started to roll the heavy table to one side, seeking a better angle. Tolly squeezed himself round the end of the bar and edged along behind it.

The next shot from the skylight struck one of the Double C cowboys defending the front of the saloon. There was a yell and the clatter of a gun being dropped as the shot man rolled over clutching at the back of his thigh.

'Bastard!'

Shay showed himself for a fraction of a second and drew fire. Again, thought Tolly. Come on, Shay, again. Shay obliged. Tolly fired for the space, aiming above and behind the rifle barrel, steadying his aim with his left hand below the right wrist.

The rifle slipped slowly through the space, finally plummeting straight down as it left its owner's fingers. There was a sighing sound and then the sniper toppled through the skylight and struck the board of the saloon with a crack that snapped his neck on impact.

The body slowly slumped onto its side and Tolly could see the wound high in the man's chest where his .45 slug had struck him.

'Fine, Tolly,' said Shay.

Tolly acknowledged the remark with a quick wave of the hand and went towards the saloon window. Paulie Yates was sitting back against the wall, a bloodied mess of flesh and bone. There was a dark red pool on the floor between his legs.

'How many?'

The cowboy at the window glanced round. 'Couple over the road still; few more down the street. Maybe we took the guts out of 'em.'

Tolly nodded. 'Maybe. Like they did to Paulie.'

Shay heard and called across. 'That shotgun, Tolly. See if there's any buckshot down behind that counter too. That'd work for us real fine.'

Tolly nodded, smiled and went over to the bar, keeping low. He found the box of buckshot. And a bottle of whisky. He unscrewed the cap and took a swig, moving his head aside when the spirit burned the back of his throat, then coughed and belched.

'Here, Shay. Catch!'

Tolly threw another bottle over to where the big cowboy was crouching. Shay caught it left-handed and called his thanks. If they were going to be there for a while, they might as well enjoy it as best they could.

In the more salubrious surroundings of The Cattlemen's House, Jed Herne was feeling pretty much the same. Most of the other customers were clustered around the doorway, or standing two or three thick on the balconies above, straining their eyes into the gathering dusk and seeing what they could of the shoot-out down at the Five Aces.

The bottle of Jim Beam was close to half-way empty: Herne was feeling close to pretty good.

CHAPTER THREE

Herne saw the group of men bustle into the bar and stand in a huddle not far inside the doorway. Men in suits for the most part; hair brushed and moustaches clipped, boots in best leather—store owners, bankers, cattle buyers, likely a minister—members of the town council. Herne recognised them and despised them for what they were. Businessmen who would do anything to preserve the peace as long as that peace was necessary to the continuance of their trade.

They'd buy your gun and sing your praises until you'd done their dirty work for them; then they'd pay you off with as little as they could and expect you to get out of town fast. Until you did, there wouldn't be another civil word and they'd do their best to make sure their wives and kids didn't even have to look on you.

Their suits were shrouds of morality that stank from fifty feet away. Herne looked away and cleaned out his mouth with another shot of Jim Beam.

He could wait: he knew what they wanted: knew they would come to him sooner or later. He read the writing on the bourbon label yet again, though by now he could have recited it by heart. He'd seen that label a lot of times.

A lot of towns.

Towns with solid names like Dodge City, religious names like Corpus Christi, names that rang with their own past like Cheyenne—towns with fancy names like Liberation.

Every one the damned same.

'That's him. That's the feller up there.'

Herne recognised the voice of the old timer from the livery stable before he picked him out. He was standing at the edge of the circle of councillors, scratching at his head with one hand and pointing up at Herne's booth with the other.

After several minutes discussion, two of the group detached themselves from the rest and walked towards Herne, making their approach as dignified as they could.

Jed Herne wanted to laugh in their faces. Instead he gave a sort of snort and pushed his chair back onto its rear legs.

The first to speak was wearing a blue wool suit that was a couple of sizes too big for him, making him look especially ludicrous. There was a patterned cravat at his neck, held in place with a diamond pin the size of a two bit piece.

'Good day to you, mister. Allow me to introduce myself and my friend. My name is Quentin Faulkner and I am the manager of this establishment.' He gestured around himself, podgy pink hand emerging from the deep sleeve of his coat. 'This here is Wilbur Merz. Mister Merz is head of the Bank of Liberation. We are rep . . .'

Herne sat forward and slammed his boot on the floor: 'A hundred dollars.'

Faulkner stared open mouthed, not used to being interrupted at any time and certainly not by someone who looked as much a no-account as Jed Herne. Merz stood with one hand on his swelling belly and the other to his jaw where it was making certain his mouth didn't drop all the way to his chest.

'Look,' Faulkner finally managed. 'Look here, I don't know what . . .'

'Hundred dollars. And ammunition.'

'It seems to me you're being more than a little presumptuous,' said the banker.

'An' it seems to me you two buzzards are bein' more that a little long-winded. A hundred dollars. And ammunition. And you can forget about my hotel bill when I leave.'

'Sir, I . . .' expostulated Faulkner.

'Really, this is . . .' protested Merz.

'Suit yourselves,' said Herne and stared past them at the rest of the town council who were standing off and trying to listen to as much of the conversation as they could. A good few other people were watching closely, suddenly interested in the tall, mean-looking stranger who was the subject of the official visitation.

Faulkner cleared his throat; Merz massaged his stomach and shifted from one foot to the other and back again. 'It seems to me that we've got off to this rather badly,' Faulkner tried.

'While it is true that we were going to make you a proposition,' said Wilbur Merz, 'we hadn't anticipated that you would be so, er, positive and, er, direct with your demands.'

'I just bet you didn't,' smiled Herne and aimed for the brass cuspidor that was standing on the floor beyond the end of the booth. He only half-hit.

Merz watched fascinated as the dark spittle dangled lower and lower from the rim. Faulkner unbuttoned his coat, then buttoned it up again.

They were still standing there, saying nothing, when a third man pushed his way between them. Six foot tall and thin as a whip. Short dark hair with a thick streak of white going through it on the right side. A three-piece suit in black and a silver watch that hung from a wide silver chain across his waistcoat. A lean face with a prominent nose and brown eyes that looked straight at a man, not around him.

Long fingers snapped open the front of the watch.

'How long you two goin' to waste everyone's time here?'

'Hastings, I resent that.'

'Faulkner, you resent every damn thing that anyone ever says or does less you do it yourself. Only trouble with that is, you never seem to do anything that really amounts to anything. How this place keeps making the money it does I never understand. You must have some mighty smart folk working on your payroll.'

Clifford Hastings sat opposite Herne and poured him a shot of his own bourbon.

'Ben Hastings,' he introduced himself, offering his hand. Herne noticed the firmness of the bony fingers and the fact that the man's eyes never stopped looking at him while they shook hands. 'I run one of the two big ranches round here. The Broken Bar, over towards the North Platte river.'

'Jed Herne. Pleased to know you.'

Hastings turned his head and called for another glass and a fresh bottle. The other two businessmen hovered around for a few moments, then walked back to where the rest of the council were waiting.

'Don't know how much you've heard of what's going on, so I'll fill you in. Some of the Double C boys are holed up in the Five Aces down the street. One of 'em killed the barber and then did the same for Bill Crompton—he was the deputy marshal. Since then they've accounted for three more and wounded a couple of others. I reckon we got one of them, maybe two. Leaves four or five.'

Herne nodded. 'Go on.'

'Folk round here are better than most in backing up the law, but now I reckon they've had enough. No sense in throwing lives away when it ain't achievin' anything.'

'Specially when you can get someone else to throw his away for you.'

Hasting's eyes moved to Herne's Colt .45. 'You ain't above selling that?'

'Already made my terms clear.'

'Make them clear to me.'

'Hundred dollars, ammunition and board.'

Hastings held out his hand again. 'You've got it.'

Herne looked over at the town council. 'What about them?'

Hastings laughed with contempt. 'Don't worry. They'll do what I say.'

Herne raised an eyebrow. 'You must find that mighty convenient?'

'Times.'

'An' these boys being from one of the other ranches—that wouldn't have nothin' to do with your eagerness to let me at 'em, would it?'

The rancher sat back and smiled: 'There's no love lost between the Double C and myself. But I didn't ask them to come in here and start shooting up the town.'

'One more thing?'

'Yes?'

'This marshal who got himself killed, you said he was the deputy. Where's the head man?'

'Out of town looking for some cattle rustlers. Won't be back till morning.'

Herne stood up; Hastings faced him. 'They wouldn't be your cattle the marshal's out lookin' for, would they?'

'Guess they would,' the rancher agreed. 'I guess they would.'

Herne spun the chambers of his Colt Peacemaker, weighing the pistol in the palm of his right hand. The grip of walnut was polished to a dull shine by constant use, the natural grain of the wood only just evident through the darkening effect of a man's hand. The long barrel, half an inch over seven inches, had a fine metallic sheen.

Oiled and ready: a precision instrument that only required the hand of an expert to make it into a killing machine.

Jed Herne dropped the gun into its holster. Paused. Drew it out, smooth and fast, pleased with the ease with which it cleared the leather.

He checked the thong at his thigh for the right degree of tightness; rested his palm on the end of the butt once more. All right: oiled and ready.

Herne stepped out from The Cattlemen's House and began to pace down the boardwalk, keeping on the opposite side of the street to The Five Aces. When he came level with the barber shop, he looked in through the shattered plate-glass window, then down at the speckles of blood that stained the wood outside.

Even in the dusk, they showed up plain, amongst the fragments of broken glass that were still littered there. Herne stepped on until he was almost level with the saloon, waiting a moment by a wagon that was outside the dry goods store. Above, the windows that had been used for firing from at the saloon were smashed and empty.

Herne glanced up and down the street. He was alone.

Though in the darkness of windows and doorways the townsfolk were waiting to see who would be killed and by whom. How many graves to add to the cemetery on the hill to the south of town, marked or unmarked depending.

'You boys in there hear me?'

Silence. Then: 'Who the hell are you?'

'Name's Herne. I bin deputised to bring you out of there.'

Another pause and—'How you aimin' to do that?'

'Two ways I know of. You can throw out your guns and come walkin' out peaceful. In which case I'll take you up the jail. What happens after that's no business of mine. Other way is, I'll come in and get you.'

'By yourself?'

'Don't see it needin' anyone else.'

Inside the darkened saloon, Shay and Tolly exchanged glances. 'You know who he is?'

Tolly shrugged his shoulders. 'What'd he say his name was? Herne? No name I know.'

'Maybe you'd do better if'n you did.'

The two cowboys turned their heads. It was one of the old men, walking slowly towards them from the back of the room. 'I knowed a man called Herne. Herne the Hunter folks called him. Fastest thing with a gun I ever see. Faster'n Earp, Jimmy Ringo, any of 'em. Thought he was dead.'

'Then maybe he is. Who's to say this feller outside's him?'

'It ain't a chance I'd like to live on.'

'Nobody's askin' you to, old man,' snapped Tolly. 'You mind your own damned business and get back over where you belong.'

'I was only warnin' yous for your own good, I . . .'

Tolly lashed out with the barrel of his gun. The old man's head rocked back. The gun sight had drawn a line across his wrinkled face. Shaking fingers went to the bloodied cut and old eyes wavered and watered nervously.

'Damn, Tolly! Weren't no need for that.'

Tolly scowled at Shay and ducked over to the window, poking his pistol round the edge of the frame. 'You there, mister deputy?'

'I'm here. Still waitin' fer your answer.'

Tolly fired twice in quick succession, aiming for the source of the sound. Neither was effective. Herne waited a few moments, then repeated his warning: 'Throw out your guns and walk out with your hands grabbing sky. Else I'm comin' in.'

'You reckon he is that Herne the Hunter?' asked one of the cowboys.

'Shit!' said Tolly. 'What difference if he is? There's four of us, ain't there? You reckon one man's gonna bust in here against the lot of us?'

'Guess not,' the Double C man replied. But he didn't sound too convinced.

'You makin' me come for you?' asked Herne a final time.

Shay moved to the door: 'That's the way it has to be.'

Herne nodded to himself; he hadn't expected anything else. In their position he'd likely have done the same. There wasn't a whole lot of choice. But at least he'd tried to talk them out—now he was going to have to earn his hundred dollars the hard way.

He slipped further back into the shadows.

Ten minutes passed. In The Cattlemen's House, the silver watch in Hastings' hands elegantly ticked out the seconds. In The Five Aces, the gambler glanced from time to time at the smaller, less expensive watch he kept in his pocket. Every time he did so, his arm shook and disturbed the chair to his right, one of the several he was shielding himself with. The deringer was still in the holster inside his sleeve and after seeing what had happened to the bartender, he had no intention of using it. Not unless there was no alternative.

'What's that slippery bastard playing at?' snarled Tolly.

'Maybe he ain't comin' in at all. Maybe it was nothin' more than a play to trick us out. Now it ain't worked, he's gone off and ain't comin' back.'

'Yea, maybe he's not this Herne the Hunter the old feller was on about at all. What d'you reckon, Tolly?'

But Tolly was remembering the man he had faced up to outside the livery stable earlier that day and he was keeping his thoughts to himself. Too clearly he recalled the way the big man's manner had made him back down—and that wasn't something Tolly had ever done in his life before.

'Hey, Tolly! You hear me?'

'Shut up!'

From the doorway, Shay looked into the saloon. 'Gettin' so dark out in that damned street we soon won't be able to see who's coming at us. I . . .'

There was a loud crash as one of the bat-wing doors was knocked open and something flew past Shay and landed about ten feet into the room.

Hey, what the . . . !'

'Jesus, that's . . . !'

The kerosene lamp was smothered at its base with old rags that had been soaked in spirit. For a second it glowed and then burst upwards into a billow of orange flame.

'Get rid of that bastard thing!'

'Kick it out!'

'Smother it!'

Shay hesitated by the doorway, uncertainly; one of the cowboys went close to the blaze, holding his coat out in front of him as if about to drop it on the flames.

'Christ!' The bullet ploughed into Shay's shoulder almost before he heard the sound of the Colt being fired. He staggered sideways, trying to bring up his own gun. Herne fired once more through the gap in the doors and then jumped through the window.

He rolled over in a half-somersault and came up into a crouch with the Colt .45 levelling up at the big Double C man's chest. Shay did his best to get a shot off but he wasn't fast enough and now he wasn't about to get any more time to practise.

Herne's bullet drove him backwards and down onto his knees. His eyes were open and he was looking at Herne as though he wanted to remember Jed's face for ever. Which likely he did—his forever didn't amount to more than a minute or so of gasped breath and bitter, bitter pain.

And it was Tolly and the cowboy's bad-tempered recklessness that he was bitter about more than anything else.

Herne didn't waste any more time on Shay. As soon as his shot had struck home, he whirled round and snapped off another in the direction of the cowboy making a dash for cover at the side of the saloon.

The shell smashed the running man's left elbow and brought him to a halt; he turned round to face Herne, right hand clutching his ruined arm.

Herne shot him between the eyes.

'Bastard!'

Jed heard the shout, the following shot, sensed something streak past his head and dived for the same table that Shay had used for a shield earlier.

He reached down to his belt and reloaded his Colt.

'Murderin' bastard! Killer!'

'One of you did his own killin' out there earlier. Started all this off.'

'That ain't the same.'

'Don't seem no different to me. 'Sides, you had your chance to come out and you didn't take it.'

Herne's gun was ready; he had picked out where the remaining two cowboys were. One behind the bar, towards the far end, he reckoned; the other about half way down, beyond the fire, back of a stack of chairs. He knew there were three others in the room but they were keeping well out of things and he wasn't bothered with them.

He rocked the table to one side, then back. The one behind the bar didn't rise to the bait. The other one did. There was a crack of a pistol shot and Herne fired one back but missed. The stench of smoke and burning wood was strong now and the centre of the saloon floor was well alight. It sent high, flickering shadows around the room, casting patterns of chair backs and table ends onto the walls.

Herne could suddenly detect a smell of burning flesh and realised that the second man he had shot had fallen into the arc of fire.

Something would have to be done soon or more of the place would catch and it would be too late. He could hear excited, loud voices from the street and the sound of a hand bell summoning the town fire force.

Herne moved his table and drew another shot in his direction. Whoever was down behind the bar was still keeping quiet—it occurred to Herne that he might have taken a stray bullet.

'I'm getting out of here. I'm not being burn . . .'

The gambler jumped up from his cover under the chairs and madè a panicked dash for the door. He was skirting the fire and making as much ground as he could when the cowboy at the end of the room shot him in the back. Herne voted the gambler his thanks and shot away a sizeable chunk of the Double C man's face.

Then he pushed the heavy table before him and leapt through the edge of the flames. Tolly saw him coming at the last moment and brought up the sawed-off shotgun.

Herne recognised the movement of the barrels and threw himself to the floor fast. He winced in spite of himself as the loads of buckshot were unleashed only a couple of feet over his head.

He reached up both hands and grabbed the end of the weapon and pulled it free from Tolly's grip. He hurled it away and used his left hand to vault the bar counter.

His right leg met Tolly trying to free his pistol from its holster. There was a shout and Tolly went back into the shelves of bottles and glasses. Herne drew his Colt and twice brought the butt down on Tolly's head as he bounced forwards. With his other hand he took Tolly's gun and pushed it into his own belt. Slowly he released the hammer of the Colt: there wasn't any point in killing him. Not now. Somebody else could have that pleasure.

Herne dragged the cowboy's body round the bar and towards the door, nearly colliding with the two old timers and the stunned youth who still wasn't sure if he was in the middle of a nightmare.

A line of men was gathered outside the saloon, some of them holding a length of hose; a little further off more men were standing by a hand pump set on a wagon. Several people held lanterns high and, by the light of one of these, Herne saw Hastings and the members of the town council.

'Right,' said Herne, 'I done my job. Now you get to

yours, before that whole place goes up.'

He dumped Tolly's unconscious body on the street before them. 'Reckon now you can take care of him yourself.'

Herne strode through the still-thickening crowd, eager for one more drink and a good night's sleep between clean sheets. He felt in need of a treat.

CHAPTER FOUR

The pendulum of the tall clock swung rhythmically from side to side behind its glass front. Above it the ornate hands showed the time to be something short of eight o'clock.

Herne sat at the table to one side of the bar and broke off a piece of bread; he began to wipe it round his plate, mopping up the juices of the steak he had just finished, together with the remaining traces of egg yolk.

Whatever else they did in The Cattlemen's House, they sure did a good breakfast.

Herne had slept well, dropping off with the noises of the night's excitement still rising up from the street. His Colt had hung in its holster from the bed post to the right of his head and he had jammed a chair underneath the door handle. Not that he was expecting any special trouble, but after a shooting there were always likely to be those coming round to make a complaint. Relatives, friends, even employers. And the nature of their complaint usually involved gunplay.

But when he had woken, the chair had not been tried, his Colt not needed. He eased himself from between the smooth sheets and poured water from the white jug into its matching bowl. The hot water he had ordered the night before had been waiting for him outside the door—something else they did well at The Cattlemen's House. Hastings had been right about Faulkner having efficient people working for him.

Herne whistled softly to himself while he shaved, feeling the hunger rising in his stomach. A good night's rest, a clean shave, a fine breakfast—what else could a man ask for?

Soon, thought Herne, Faulkner or one of the others would be coming to him with his hundred dollars. That would just about round things off well. Likely he'd then collect his horse and ride down to Cheyenne. With the close of spring, there'd be trail herds moving in there a-plenty. Down the Western Trail from Montana Territory above the Yellowstone; up the Goodnight-Loving Trail that came north through New Mexico. All heading for the railroad and the chance to sell their herds for a fine price before they were shipped east on the Union Pacific to Chicago.

A lot of cattle: a lot of men.

Herne knew that meant trouble and trouble meant work as far as he was concerned. Yes, he'd head down towards Cheyenne soon as he'd collected his dues.

'More coffee?'

Herne turned his head. The woman was close to thirty, dark brown hair held down round her face with pins, a mouth that could have been a little more generous, eyes that seemed to change from brown to blue then back again.

'I heard what you done yesterday. Getting them killers like that. You must be some man.'

She was smiling down at him, holding the coffee pot with one hand, letting the other rest immediately below her hip.

Herne nodded pleasantly but said nothing.

She gestured with the pot: 'You want some more?'

'Sure. Why not?'

She came closer and leaned over the table at Herne's side, letting her arm graze his shoulder as she poured the dark, hot liquid into Herne's cup. As she straightened, he was aware of her hip pressing against him for a moment.

Then she was standing at the far side of the table. 'Anything else you want, while you're here ... you only have to ask.' She parted her lips and Herne saw the tip of her pink tongue. 'Man like you.'

Herne grinned in spite of himself. 'Real nice of you. Only thing is, don't reckon I'll be stayin' long.'

She pouted. 'That's a shame.' Shrugged her shoulders. 'Still, that's what happens, seems to me.'

'How's that?'

'Oh, I don't know, folk hurryin' from one place to another so fast, just to keep on the move. Never settlin'. You must know how it is.'

The clock behind Herne began to strike the hour.

'Sure,' he said. 'I know the way it is.'

'Well ...' She hung her head to one side and a length of brown hair slipped out from under its pin and trailed down. '... if you change your mind, my name's Josie.'

Herne nodded again and watched her as she walked away. Something about the sway of her hips ...

He lifted his cup and sipped at the coffee: it was hot and strong and slightly bitter.

Quentin Faulkner was wearing a different coloured suit but it had obviously been made by the same tailor. He strutted across the floor of The Cattlemen's House, with his own self-importance shining in his eyes. The pin holding his cravat in place was the same; the cravat had been changed to match the suit.

He stopped a couple of feet away from the table where Herne was sitting and reached into his coat pocket for a white envelope.

'Mister Herne, the town council have asked me to give you this on their behalf.' And he leaned forward with the envelope held lightly between his round, scrubbed fingers.

Herne grunted thanks and the envelope was dropped onto the table. Faulkner turned to go.

'Hold on now.'

'Mister Herne, my business with you is over.'

'Not quite yet it ain't.'

Faulkner tugged at one of the lapels of his coat. 'I assure you, sir, that it is. I can only hope that you will saddle up and leave Liberation as soon as possible. Good day, sir.'

Herne was out of his seat and round the table quicker than Faulkner considered possible. Only the hand that held him fast by his collar made him know otherwise.

'What's the all-fired hurry?'

'Nuh . . . uh . . .'

With the pressure on his throat, Faulkner was finding communication difficult.

'Come back here and sit down. Take some coffee.'

He whirled the man round and pushed him over to the table; pulled up a chair and shoved him down into it.

'Josie!'

She came running, with a flurry of skirt and petticoats.

'Your boss wants some coffee.'

'I don't . . .' he blurted, trying to rise.

'He does,' countered Herne, pushing him back so hard that the chair rocked and nearly spilled Faulkner onto the ground. 'He surely does.'

While Josie poured them both cups of coffee, Herne held the envelope in his hand, staring across at Faulkner, who was squirming inside the plentiful material of his suit. Josie managed to get the coffee into the cups without her face cracking into too broad a smile, then retreated.

'Drink it.'

'But . . .'

'Drink!'

Faulkner drank, the liquid slipping down one side of

his mouth as he fidgeted in his chair, now looking at Herne, now glancing round towards the door.

'Expecting somebody?'

'No.'

'When's that marshal of yours get back into town?'

Faulkner gulped in air. 'I . . . I don't know.'

'Hastings around?'

Faulkner shook his head. 'He went back out to his ranch.'

'Uh-huh.'

Herne pushed a finger underneath the flap of the envelope and slit it across. Then he took out the folded bills and placed them on the table. Faulkner looked at the door with increasing desperation.

'Might as well count 'em.'

Herne began to separate the notes, then count them out slowly onto the table. As he did so, his mouth set firm, his eyes grew hard and set.

'Sixty dollars.' The voice was quiet and low but clear enough to be heard all round the almost empty room.

An old man who was wiping the counter of the horse-shoe bar looked up and stopped work, the cloth bunched in his hand. Another ceased emptying the cuspidors and began slowly to back away in the direction of the door.

In the kitchen, Josie hung up her apron and came towards the hatch.

'Sixty dollars.'

Faulkner sweated; ground his hands together, fingers against palms; did his best to avoid Herne's stare. Herne held up the bills for him to see, then let them fall.

'Where's the rest?'

Faulkner shook his head. He opened his mouth as if to speak, but no words came out.

'I'll give you ten seconds to answer.'

Herne stood up and for Faulkner his shape seemed to fill the room.

'. . . eight . . . nine . . .'

'No! I ... we ... we thought ... the fire ...'

'What about the fire?'

'The damage. The cost of fixing the damage to the saloon. We ...'

'To hell with what you and your bunch of schemin' friends thought! We had a deal.'

'You made the deal with Hastings.'

'An' you agreed to it.'

'Yes, but there was no talk about setting fire to places.'

'An' nothin' that said not to. Nothin' about damage to property. I went in an' did the job best way I saw it. Took four men for you an' stopped them shootin' up any more of your precious citizens. That was what you wanted wasn't it?'

'Yes, but ...'

'And that was what I did, wasn't it?'

'Yes, but ...'

'Then hand over the rest of my money.'

Faulkner pushed himself up in the chair, still hoping someone would come into the place and intervene on his behalf. He sighed and gulped like a fish out of water and tried to make a run for it. He didn't come near to succeeding. Herne grabbed his arm and hoisted him back, tightening his grip until Faulkner's face was a contorted mask.

'You give me the forty dollars. You can get it back from the council later.'

'What if they don't see it that way?'

'Then you lost yourself forty dollars.'

Faulkner tried again and Herne tripped him and lifted him high over his own head, both arms outstretched and taking his weight with ease. He started to shake Faulkner up and down until his belongings began to fall out of his pockets.

When he saw the wallet on the floor, Herne turned the man over fast and sat him back down in the chair where he held on tight and tried to rid his head of dizziness.

Herne picked up the wallet and counted out twenty dollars in one dollar bills.

'This all you got?'

Faulkner looked up at him, bemused.

Herne stuffed the notes into his pocket and grinned: 'Let's try that office of yours fer the rest.'

The safe was behind a picture on the wall behind Faulkner's desk. Built in real fancy. Herne watched as Faulkner's fingers fumbled with the lock.

'Fetch that box out and set it down easy.'

The box was metal, painted black with gold lines over it. Faulkner set it on the surface of his desk like it might explode.

'Open it up.'

There were several rolls of bills inside, close to five hundred dollars, Herne reckoned. He stood there with his hand held out, waiting for Faulkner to count off the remaining twenty dollars he was due.

When the notes were safe in his pocket he laughed and suddenly Faulkner was staring down the barrel of a Colt .45.

'What are you ... what are you aimin' to do here?'

'Lot of money to keep in a little old safe like that. Asks to be taken. What's the matter with the bank here in town? Don't you trust that banker friend of yours to look after your cash for you or somethin'?'

Faulkner collapsed backwards into his chair, unable to look Herne in the face and fearing the worst. Herne swivelled the Colt round on his finger and let it slide down into the holster on his hip.

'So long, Faulkner. An' let me give you a bit of advice. Next time you need to hire a gun, make sure you deal with him fair an' square. Lest you end up with that gun comin' after you.'

Herne went out of the office and shut the door firmly

behind him. Josie was standing outside the kitchen, hands on hips, her face half anxious, half smiling.

'He's been needing that for a long time. Only there weren't the man around who could do it.'

'Maybe so.'

Herne went to step past her, but she moved in front of him and placed a hand on his chest, fingers spread. 'Other things needin' doing—other things there weren't a man around big enough to handle.'

Herne looked down at her: the eyes were blue now and staring up into his; the pressure of the fingers against him was certain and warm; he could smell her breath, the odour of her body.

He put his hand up to hers and held her wrist for a moment, not hurting her but not gentle either. 'I got to get my things. Move on.' He shifted her hand away and she stepped aside.

When he looked back from the stairs she had gone—just the two bent old men cleaning the saloon, that and the swinging of the pendulum, the ticking of the clock.

'Herne! Jed Herne!'

Inside the room, Herne spun round, hand already covering the butt of his gun. The shout had come from downstairs in the saloon.

'Come on down here with your hands well in sight.'

He moved closer to the door, careful not to stand directly behind it.

'Who is that?'

'This is the marshal.'

Herne blinked, opened and closed the fingers of his right hand, making the knuckles crack; he lifted the Colt clear and checked and spun the chambers. He dropped the gun back into place and turned the handle of the door.

Three paces along the corridor, then two to the head

of the stairs. The marshal of Liberation stood back from the bottom of the stairs and his pistol wasn't in its holster at all.

CHAPTER FIVE

The gun the marshal favoured was the same as Herne's—a Colt Peacemaker .45. Right now it was in his hand and pointing at an angle up the stairs; an angle that made it plumb in line with Herne's chest. As Herne stood there, looking down, the marshal thumbed back the hammer and in the stillness of the saloon the triple click rang out clearly, breaking the rhythm of the clock's continuous ticking.

Herne looked the man over. The Colt wasn't the only gun he was wearing. A gun belt ran diagonally across his chest with a holster close to the right arm pit. The Remington Frontier .44 with the black wood butt was ready for a left-handed cross-draw. A couple of feet to the marshal's right, leaning against one of the tables, was a Remington ten-gauge shotgun with 28-inch double barrels.

Not a man who believed in taking chances.

The marshal was in his early twenties, Herne guessed. Wearing black pants and a black shirt, with a black waistcoat. Only thing that broke up the colour was the silver marshal's badge on his chest—opposite his second gun.

His face was handsome—more than most—with a neat brown moustache and unwavering eyes. The only thing that maybe marred it was the small, round, purple birthmark on his right cheekbone.

Herne had made no further move; his hand was still as far from his own gun.

'Want to see me, marshal?'

'That's right.'

'What's the trouble?'

'Got this complaint. Seems you robbed one of our citizens of some of his money.'

'That so?'

'Uh-huh. Emptied his wallet and then forced him to open his safe and took some of that, too.'

Herne shook his head from side to side slowly.

'You believe everythin' you hear, marshal?'

'Depends who's tellin' it.'

There was more than a scattering of folk in The Cattlemen's House by now. Crowded close to the door and round the curve of the bar; a few on the flight of stairs that went up behind Herne to the second storey. He could see Josie close by the entrance to the kitchen, her hands fiddling with an apron. Quentin Faulkner stood just inside his office with the door barely open.

'What you aimin' t' do 'bout it?' Herne asked.

'Take you in. Talk about it in my office. I'm a man as likes to listen to both sides of things.'

'That a fact?'

Herne stepped off the landing and onto the top step, then down another, and another. The marshal let his body fall deeper into a crouch, the gun shifting slightly to cover Herne's new position.

'That's far enough!'

Herne stopped, letting his right hand swing to within an inch of his Colt.

'Last man tried that bought himself a wooden box. He thought he was pretty fast, too.'

Herne stared down, eyes narrowed.

'Tell you what—'fore you come any further, just ease that gun out and let me have it.'

Herne almost smiled. 'You want this gun?'

'Uh-huh.'

Herne's right hand began to move—

'No!'

Stopped moving, resting on the worn butt.

'Use the left hand, fingers only, keep the other one high. That's it. Lift her out real slow.'

Herne reached in front of his body with his left hand and did as the marshal said. The Colt was back to front in his left hand.

'You sure you want this?'

'I'm sure.'

Herne lobbed the gun through the air, right over where the marshal stood. Without effort, the man put up his free hand and caught it, glanced at it quickly, then pushed it down into his belt.

'That sure makes you a regular arsenal, don't it?' said Herne.

'Maybe it does. But I feel safer this way.'

He took a step to one side and dropped his own pistol back into its holster. He lifted up the shotgun and covered Herne the rest of the way down the stairs.

'Okay. Let's walk us across the street. And remember I'll be right behind you with this.'

Herne nodded: 'I ain't about to forget.'

They went through the crowd of onlookers round the door and stepped out of sight. Both Josie and Faulkner watched them go with great interest—and only one of them was smiling.

The marshal pushed the door of his office shut by leaning back on it and stacked the shotgun against the wall by his left hand. He reached for the gun he had taken from Herne and looked down at it, glancing over at where Herne stood in the middle of the room.

'Catch!'

He threw the gun with his right hand and as it was in the air he made his cross-draw with his left. As Herne snatched his Colt out of the air, the marshal had the

Remington snug in his hand, hammer cocked.

'Damn!' said Herne. 'You sure got good on that one.'

'Guess I did at that.' The marshal held his expression for a few seconds longer, then his face cracked into a wide smile and he reholstered the gun.

'Jed Herne! Never thought I'd get to see you again. Not in these parts.'

'An' not with me starin' down the end of that gun of yorn.'

'Sorry 'bout that, Jed.'

'Plumb glad it was you an' no one else.'

'If it had, what would you have done different?'

Herne shrugged. 'Let's wait till that happens and see.' He went forward to where the marshal was standing and clapped both hands to his shoulders. 'How are you, Dan? Sure lookin' good.'

Marshal Dan Stewart nodded. 'Okay, I guess. Nothin's ever perfect.'

'Got trouble?'

'Who ain't?'

Stewart went over to his desk and took a tin of tobacco from a drawer, found some papers and started to roll a cigarette. Herne watched as the slender fingers expertly manipulated the paper. 'Want one?' he offered.

'No, thanks.' Herne sat on the edge of the desk. 'Want to talk about it?'

Stewart lit the cigarette and drew the smoke down into his lungs; waited until he had breathed out. 'Got this little matter to settle first.'

'Faulkner, you mean?'

'Yep.'

'You ain't treatin' that serious, are you?'

'He's a mighty important man around here.'

Herne stiffened. 'You mean when he shouts you go ahead and jump?'

Stewart looked at him closely, not hiding the fact that Herne's remark had stung. 'That's not the way I'd see it.'

'Maybe not. But then again, perhaps it's Hastings who calls your tune.'

Stewart jumped up and glared down at Herne, the birth mark on his cheek showing more brightly than ever. 'What the hell's got into you, Jed, one minute you're pleased to see me again, the next you're accusin' me of being in the pocket of every big man in the territory.'

Herne put up a hand to calm him down. 'Shit, Dan, you're right. Maybe I'm talkin' way out of line. But look at it my way—when I got here yesterday these cowboys were shootin' up the place while you were out lookin' fer Hastings' cattle. Today, soon as you get back, Faulkner comes runnin' to you an' right off you come fer me tooled-up like a small army.'

'Didn't know it was you when I called you out.'

'He didn't say my name?'

'No. Reckoned maybe I'd've thought twice 'bout comin' for you if'n I'd known who you was.'

Herne looked at the younger man keenly: 'And would you?'

'Like you said earlier, wait till it happens an' then we'll see.'

Stewart drew deeply on his cigarette. 'If you don't want one of these, could you use a cup of coffee?'

Herne relaxed: 'Sure,' he said. 'Sure.'

First time he'd met Dan Stewart it had been a couple of years back. Stewart had been marshal of a place called Ogden then. Right off he'd impressed Jed by the way he handled himself—the way he handled other people. Firm and sure but not too pushy. Way he took care of things with those guns of his had been pretty impressive as well.

Only after a while had Herne found out the young lawman's name and then that he'd known his old man years further back. John Stewart—Long John, they'd called him. He and Jed had roped horses together for a while;

chased wild herds high up into the hills of Montana, nothing around them but sun and sky, nothing below them but rock.

'Seen your pa lately?' Herne asked after Dan Stewart had handed him an enamel mug of coffee.

'Saw him four months back. He's livin' east of here now. Omaha way.'

'How's he doin'?'

'Okay . . . 'cept for one thing?'

'What's that?'

'Lost his sight round Christmas. Stone blind.'

Herne looked closely at the movement of the liquid in his mug as he tilted it first one way and then the other. Horses, wagons, boots went past the door outside. Neither man spoke for some time.

Then: 'Want to tell me 'bout this business with Faulkner's money?'

Jed told him.

'Seems you was in the right to me. Faulkner was withholding what was your due.'

'And you'll tell him that?' Herne questioned.

'I'll tell him just that. You got my word on it.'

Herne set down his mug and started to move towards the door.

'That business down at The Five Aces—you handled that real well. Thanks.'

'I got paid.' He set his hand to the door handle. 'You seen the one I brought in?'

Stewart nodded towards the door that led to the cells. 'He's in there, hollerin' off at the mouth how I got to let him out real soon or else the whole of the Double C'll be bustin' in here and settin' him free.'

'Any truth in that, you reckon?'

'Could be. Specially if'n they find out it was Hastings sent you in after 'em. Double C hate Hastings an' the Broken Bar worse than rattler poison.'

'It them bin takin' Broken Bar stock?'

Stewart shrugged. 'Could be. But if'n it is, I sure can't prove it. Not yet, anyways.'

Herne nodded and opened the door.

'Jed.'

Herne looked at him, waiting.

'You got to move on right off? You got work lined up or something?'

'Could have. Why?'

'Deputy got shot yesterday. I know that ain't much of a job for a man like you, but . . . hell, Jed, truth is, I could use someone like you about now. Someone I can trust. This territory's 'bout to bust itself wide open an' I don't know if I can hold it down as one man.'

Herne hesitated, thinking. 'What's the pay, Dan?'

'Eighty a month and ammunition. There's a place you can sleep back of the cells. Hell, I know it ain't much, but . . .'

'Tell you what. I'll go down to the livery stable and check out that stallion of mine. Maybe take a ride out a-ways. Come back to town fer a bite to eat. Think it over. I'll let you know this afternoon.'

'Fair enough, Jed. You do things as you see best.'

Herne stepped out onto the boardwalk and shut the office door behind him. There were three wanted posters pinned to the wall outside, one for rustling, two for murder. One of the killers wasn't more than fifteen.

He waited while a pair of women in black dresses walked slowly past him, pretending not to be interested in who the stranger was who had shot all those men the night before.

Then he walked on down the street towards the livery stable. It took him ten minutes to get away from the old timer who worked there, having to listen to several different versions of what had happened in The Five Aces, each more gory than the one before. By the end of it he didn't recognise the scene himself and he was the one who'd been in there. It was like one of them stories they wrote back east about Buffalo Bill Cody and suchlike.

Least no one was going to write a book about him.

Around one Herne walked into The Cattlemen's House. Quentin Faulkner was taking a drink at the bar and he nearly choked on his own whisky.

'What are you doing here? Why aren't you in jail?'

'As for that,' said Herne, 'you'd better ask the marshal. For the first part, I'm here 'cause you had the sense to hire yourself a good cook.'

'But I insist . . .'

Herne let the owner see the gun at his hip. 'You insist nothin'. Any time you don't fancy my custom in this place of yours you try throwin' me out.'

And he strode past him towards the tables at the back where food was being served.

'Thought you was leaving?' said Josie as she set the plate of steak, potatoes and eggs before him.

Herne smiled: 'Tell you what—food round here's so damned fine makes a man want to stay a while.'

Josie didn't stop grinning all the way back to the kitchen —and then some.

CHAPTER SIX

The badge on Jed Herne's shirt showed clearly as he pushed open the bat-wing doors of The Five Aces. A hurricane lamp hung from a hook close to the centre of the ceiling, moving slightly in the wind. Underneath it, two men knelt on the floor, busy replacing those boards that had got burnt up the night before.

One of the men was wearing a sweat-stained stetson, the other bare-headed and mostly bald. They looked at Herne for several moments before the bald one picked up his hammer and went back to work.

'You sure done a good job,' said the second man, the sarcasm clearly evident in his voice.

'Sorry 'bout your place.'

'I'll just bet you are.'

The bald man took a nail from his mouth and set its point against the floor. 'Take it easy, Ed. Don't rile him any.'

'Why the hell shouldn't I? What reason he have for burning this place of mine down?'

The bald man struck the nail, gently at first, then hard three times until only the rounded end showed in the board. 'It didn't burn down, for one thing. For another, things could have bin a whole lot worse if it had been left to others to try and get them bums out of here.'

'Those bums are my living,' said the saloon owner acidly.

'And you chose it,' put in Herne.

The man with the hat stood up. 'Anythin' wrong with that?'

Herne shook his head. 'Not a thing.' He raised his right hand briefly in salute. 'Be seein' you gents.'

As soon as the doors were swinging to behind Herne, the saloon owner grabbed up a hammer and flung it across the room, where it cannoned off one of the walls and into a pile of stacked chairs.

'Damn him! Comin' in here to gloat.'

'He weren't necessarily gloatin', Ed. Just checkin' us out on his rounds. Don't get so all-fired het up about it. We may be glad he's here afore long.'

'Only way I'll be glad to see him stay here is up in the cemetery.'

The bald man hammered another nail. 'Double C boys have their way you might be able to take along a wreath yet.'

An hour later Herne paused outside the saddlers and leant against the door, checking it. As he did so he heard a sound from directly across the street—someone trying to walk soft.

'Hold it!'

He was round and in a crouch, both hands extended, one holding the Colt. In the shadows opposite, the figure moved, came forward to the end of boardwalk.

'It's okay, Jed. Only me.'

Herne recognised Dan Stewart and put up his gun with relief. The two men met in the middle of the street.

'Seen anythin'?' Stewart asked.

'Nothin' to trouble us.'

'Good. Thought we might get a visit.'

'Yep. That Tolly alone in the jail?'

'For now. But there's three locks between him and the street and no back way in. He'll rest easy.'

'I reckon. What's it like up at The Cattlemen's House?'

'More crowded than usual. On account of The Five Aces being temporarily out of business, I guess. You could take a look.'

'I'll do that. See you, Dan.'

'Jed.'

Light spilled out from the windows and doors; sounds of laughter and talk; clink and clatter of glass; jangly, off-key notes from an upright piano.

When Herne went in not too many people noticed; they were too preoccupied with their own evening's entertainment. Not that Jed minded—it was better that way.

He walked round the big room, stopping every now and then to look at the spin of the faro wheel, the deal of the cards at blackjack, the bidding of the poker players. Faulkner saw him, but gave no sign of recognition.

Whatever arguments Dan Stewart had used on the town council to get him the post of deputy, they must have been pretty persuasive.

Finally Herne made his way towards the curved bar, leaning one elbow against it and looking towards the rear of the room while waiting for one of the bartenders to serve him.

There were six or seven saloon girls scattered about the place. All of them wore identical emerald green dresses with layers of black petticoat showing underneath and black edging at the sleeves and across the bodice. Black fishnet stockings and high heeled shoes.

Herne paid for his shot of bourbon.

Two brunettes, three blondes, one with hair that was jet black and one redhead—none of them anything like as attractive as the girl from the kitchen. What was her name? Josie?

He turned back to the bar, disappointed that she wasn't there and annoyed with himself for feeling that way. He had the best part of a hundred dollars in his pocket and any one—or two—of those girls in green would keep him company for as much of the night as he wanted.

Maybe, Herne thought, maybe ...

He saw the bunch come through the door out of the corner of one eye. Five, six, no, seven men. Keeping close together in the way that such gangs always did. Seeking shelter in their own noise, boosting one another's courage. They pushed and elbowed people out of the way until they had cleared a space for themselves at the bar and began calling out for whisky and beer.

Herne glanced round to see if he could see Faulkner, but the owner had slipped out of sight. Probably, thought Jed, sheltering in his office and guarding his precious safe.

Herne swallowed back his drink and moved back from the bar, putting space between himself and the group at the counter. He didn't want to make what they'd come for too easy for them—and he was certain he knew what they were after: himself.

He wondered where Dan Stewart was, whether he should just walk out and leave them to it. Before he could make up his mind, it was made up for him.

'Anyone seen that new lawman you got in this town?'

The voice was harsh, rough; even so not too many folk heard it. The first time. After the second faces began to look round, assess the situation and move away. The speaker stepped forward into the space that had cleared around him.

Herne stood alongside the blackjack table and took a good look at him. Well over six foot, a couple of inches taller than Herne himself, and built like a prize bull. His face was a mass of black stubble and thick hair fell forward over his forehead in unkempt clumps. He had a riding quirt fastened round his right wrist; a gun holstered at his left side.

Herne guessed that he was the ramrod of the Double C.

'I said, anyone seen this new marshal you got here in town?'

To Herne's left, the blackjack dealer stopped pushing forward the cards. One by one the customers forgot about their stakes, eased back their chairs and moved back into the crowd.

The redhead in emerald green picked up her skirt over one arm and hurried for safety. The piano player had stopped: the last notes hung discordantly on the thick, smoky air.

'Well, now, boys,' said the ramrod, turning his head part way to the other cowboys, 'look what we got us here. It ain't a real marshal at all—just some crumblin' old man they dressed up in a badge.'

'Yea,' said one of the others, stepping away from the bar, 'that can't be the one as took Tolly in and killed Shay an' the rest. All he's good fer is standin' guard over his own coffin.'

The Double C men laughed and Herne gave the speaker the once over. Little more than a kid, five eight or nine, spiky brown hair and an attempt at growing a moustache that was nothing but a joke. Two guns strapped to his sides and worn too low to get an even draw. He looked down the room at Herne and Jed saw that there was a cast in his right eye.

The one with the quirt took a step along the floor: 'That right you're the new deputy?'

'That's right,' answered Herne in even tones.

'You're this Herne the Hunter we bin hearin' about?'

'Some folk call me that.'

The kid stepped forward: 'That ain't what I'd call you. Not me. I'd call you a washed-up old man who don't know when he's over the hill and rollin' down the other side.'

Herne bit down on his lower lip. The crowd moved even further back, hugging the walls. Behind the horse-shoe bar, the three bartenders were quietly lifting as many of the liquor bottles below the counter as they could.

'You hear me, old man?'

'I hear you,' answered Herne, a tinge of weariness in his voice.

I hear you now, he thought, and I've heard you for the past ten years, ever since this hair of mine started to go grey and the lines came to my face. Heard you in every street and saloon between the Mississippi and the Rio Grande. Nights when I've slept bad I've heard you in my dreams.

'What you aimin' to do about it?'

Herne shrugged his broad shoulders. 'Not a damned thing,' he said and turning his back, started to walk slowly along the room, real, real slow.

The kid jumped forward, grabbed a chair and hurled it across the floor. 'You see that?' he shouted. 'You all see that? That no-account deputy crawlin' off with his tail between his legs like the mangy dog he is.'

Herne stopped: turned, hands well clear of his gun belt. The kid was standing in a gunfighter's crouch, the tips of each set of fingers inches above the polished butts of his guns. Behind him to his left, the other Double C cowboys were lined up against the bar, passing a bottle silently between them. The ramrod of the outfit stood back to the kid's right, hand close to his pistol.

Around sixty people in the saloon and every one of them watching Herne and the kid, eyes flicking nervously from one to the other.

'Right, son, you had your say. Now I'm goin' t' have mine. You run off at the mouth any more an' I'm goin' t' come down there an' take them guns away from you and ram the barrels down that stupid throat of yours.'

The kid shifted his stance, blinked, the cast in his eye more evident than ever. The men at the bar started to spread out; the bottle came to rest on the counter.

'Old man, you ain't about to do nothin'. Unless it's to crawl out of this place an' find some old kennel for the night.'

Herne drew breath and started to walk back down the room, all the way keeping his hand curved above the butt of his Colt, all the way fixing the kid with his eyes and staring at him hard.

'I'm warnin' you, old man. Don't you come one step closer or I'll drop you fer dead!'

Herne kept going.

The kid held his breath, clenched and unclenched his fingers, became aware of the sweat that was running down both sides of his face and of the nerve that ticked away at his temple. The next pace the lawman took he'd go for his guns ... the next ... the ...

'Don't you ...'

But Herne was upon him. A grip like a vice clamped down on his right arm and something that felt like falling rock thudded against his jaw. A fire shot through him as a knee was rammed between his legs and he knew he was falling backwards, knew his mouth was open wide and that what he could hear was the sound of himself screaming. Screaming with pain like some fool kid.

Herne let the boy fall away from him and, just before he hit the floor, he kicked out with his boot and caught him in the kidneys. The slight body shifted several feet in the air before it crashed against a table. Herne ducked down with both hands reaching for the twin guns at the kid's belt.

Silence in the saloon and then everyone began talking at once. Everyone except for the cowboys from the Double C. They stood there stunned. The only one of them making any sound was the whimpering shape on the floor.

Herne's Colt .45 was still in its holster.

He turned to face the man with the quirt. 'You boss of this outfit?'

'Scott Miller. I ramrod for the Double C, sure.'

'Well, next time you or any of your boys come into town lookin' to pick a fight I reckon you'd better give it a long, hard thought first. An' ...' He pointed to the ground, '... don't try to use some punk like that 'cause he's still wet behind the ears. Now drink up an' get him out of here. Throw him over his horse and take him back to your ranch.'

Miller looked Herne steadily in the face. He didn't like being talked to like that—not in front of a saloon full of people, especially not in front of his own men. But at that moment he didn't see what he was going to do about it. Herne had showed that his reputation wasn't built on rumours; had proved that what had happened back in The Five Aces hadn't been any kind of fluke.

'That understood?' asked Herne.

'Understood,' said Miller with a scowl on his dark face. 'For now.'

'What about the kid's guns?' asked one of the cowboys.

'He wants these back,' said Herne, 'he's goin' t' have t' come to me real nice and polite an' ask fer 'em. Now when he comes to, you be sure to tell him that.'

'Come on, boys, let's get out of here.'

Scott Miller shouldered his way towards the door, leaving the others to lift up the still moaning kid and carry him out into the street.

Herne stood his ground, watching in case any one of them should try something at the last moment. But they didn't. Behind him the piano started to play again and soon there was the sound of a group of horses galloping away.

Only then did Jed Herne turn round.

Only then did he spot Dan Stewart on the stairs to the back, his Remington shotgun over one arm and a smile on his face nearly as wide as a house.

Herne walked over towards him.

'How long you bin there?'

'Just before you started that walk of yorn. Snuck through the crowd when they was all watchin' you an' that fool kid.'

Herne nodded.

'Not that I thought it was anythin' you couldn't handle.

I mean, they was only half a dozen.'

'This time,' said Herne.

'Yep, this time.' Stewart slapped Herne on the arm. 'Come on, I'll buy you a drink. My badge pulls thirty a month more than yours.'

The girl with the red hair and the green dress came over to their table and tried to draw them into conversation, but Herne shook his head and Stewart gave her his best smile and sent her on her way.

'Think you an' me'll take us a ride early tomorrow,' Dan said.

Herne lifted his glass. 'Where to?'

Stewart's smile was back on his handsome face. 'Double C,' he said.

CHAPTER SEVEN

The morning air was clear and bright, with a sharpness to it that smacked a man awake. The trail that Herne and Stewart followed led them down into a valley bounded by lines of Ponderosa pine and, above those, Douglas fir. A stream meandered along the valley bottom, flecked with white spray where the water passed over rocks. Yellowing cottonwoods bordered either side of the stream, branches glowing in the early sun.

Herne sensed his horse willing to move towards the water and let it have its head. The grass between track and stream was scattered with wild flowers, yellow, purple and pink.

'Sure is a fine morning,' said Dan Stewart as the two animals drank from the stream.

'Surely is.' Herne was bending over the edge of the water, cupping it in both hands and lifting it to his mouth.

'Take a look there,' said Dan, still in the saddle.

Herne stood and looked where Stewart was pointing. A small herd of mule deer were grazing the far side of the meadow, their long ears pricking up every now and then at the sound of the men's voices.

'Now they,' said Dan, 'have got the right idea. Just wanderin' in the sun, with nothin' to do but eat an' drink. Don't even have to pay for it.'

Herne made no reply, but pulled himself back onto his horse. 'Somethin' I bin meanin' to ask, Dan. How come you left that job you had in Ogden an' come up here?'

Stewart glanced quickly at Herne, then looked away, fingers fidgetting with the rein. 'Long story, Jed.'

'An' you don't want t' tell it?'

'Sometime, maybe. Not now.' He swung his animal round and away from the water. 'We got us a job to do.'

Herne shrugged his shoulders and watched as the marshal moved away, heading back towards the trail. After a few moments, he touched his spurs lightly to his horse's side and followed.

The Double C ranch was one of the biggest in the southern part of Wyoming Territory. The ranch house had been built in such a way as to suggest it was intended to stay that way. With a background of high hills, the main building was brick built for the first two floors, with an additional wood floor and balcony set above. Some way to the right, there were a number of lesser buildings, the longest of which served as a bunkhouse for the Double C cowhands.

There was a large corral to the left of the house, with a smaller one behind it. As Stewart and Herne rode towards the buildings, a group of men were standing round the larger corral, watching as one of their number did his best to get a saddle onto one of the new stock.

Their shouts of encouragement or derision grew louder, then faded away as they became aware of the two men riding slowly towards them. Stopped altogether as they realised who the men were.

One of them set off for the main house at a run, the others leaned back against or sat on the corral rails, watching Herne and Stewart closely.

Dan kept a foot or two in front; he had told Herne to leave the initial talking to him—something that Jed was quite happy to do.

They got to within fifty yards of the ranch house before Scott Miller appeared. The ramrod came out of the house and down the short flight of steps that led to the yard at the front. The riding whip was in its usual place on his right wrist; his hair and beard were unkempt as before.

He stood there, feet apart, waiting, the end of the whip drumming impatiently against his leather boot.

The Double C cowboys watched the two lawmen go past them with hardly a word, starting to mutter once they had moved past. Herne recognised three of them from the previous night in The Cattlemen's House—the kid, though, was nowhere to be seen. Maybe he was still nursing his injuries . . . and his pride.

Dan Stewart reined in his horse fifteen yards away from Miller and Herne came up alongside him. The two men sensed some movement behind them and knew that the cowboys were adjusting their positions in case of a show-down.

'You got a lot of nerve, marshal, ridin' in here like this. Bringin' him with you.' He nodded at Herne briefly.

'Got business, Miller.'

'That so. Who with?'

'Not you. With your boss.'

'Suppose the boss don't want to see you?'

'That ain't for you to decide.'

Herne was aware of the movement of Stewart's right hand. He hoped that he wasn't going to make a play for his gun: not then and there.

The ramrod had noticed the movement, too, but did nothing about it. The whip continued to tap against his boot. 'An' if the decision's already bin made?'

'It'll have to be unmade, won't it?'

One of the cowboys came into the edge of Herne's vision; he thought he saw a piece of sacking move in one of the bunkhouse windows. Couldn't be sure, but he wasn't about to forget the possibility. Too many guns, Herne thought, too many by half.

Dan Stewart edged his horse a few paces further forward. 'You goin' t' take my message, or do I have to ride through you an' deliver it myself?'

'Marshal, you're either a bigger fool than I took you for, or you're ridin' your luck for some reason I don't understand.'

Miller's left hand was now poised over his gun, his eyes fixed on Stewart's face. Herne let his own hand rest on the butt of his Colt and pressed his knee against the rifle by his saddle. Two men to his right, five more behind, at least one in the bunkhouse and someone else up at the first floor window of the ranch house. He didn't like the odds one bit.

'Never mind who's a fool, Miller, just get inside an' tell the boss we want to have words. If'n you want to try anythin' we still got to come out once we bin in.'

Miller stopped moving his right arm and the whip ceased its tattoo. Herne tensed, knowing the ramrod had made up his mind at last. His fingers on the smooth wood of the pistol butt, he slowly exhaled as Scott Miller turned abruptly on his heel and stomped back towards the house. Miller went heavily up the steps and disappeared inside.

A couple of minutes later, he came back out. 'The boss'll see you.' He spat out the words like they were scraps of rotten food.

Herne and Stewart rode towards the rail at the side of the ranch house steps and the Double C ramrod cussed and walked over towards the bunkhouse, kicking up the dust with his boots as he went.

The hallway was larger than Herne had expected; its floorboards were polished and everything smelt of lavender. On a round table to the left of the door, a bunch of tall, blue flowers stood in a white bowl spotted with a pattern of roses. To the right, a staircase wound its way upwards; close by there was a closed white door.

Stewart took off his hat and lobbed it at one of the hooks beside the front door. It settled neatly over the metal hook and as it did so, the sound of applause came from the landing.

The two men looked round, one calmly, the other with obvious surprise.

'Hello, Dan. Have you brought your new deputy out to meet me?'

The owner of the Double C started to descend the staircase. She was dressed in a white shirt and dark green pants that fitted as though she'd been stitched into them. Her hair was long and dark, falling well past neck and shoulders. She favoured them with a smile that was as bright and cold as the Spring air had been when they'd started their ride out from town.

She took Dan Stewart's hand and held it for a moment or two longer than was necessary. 'It's been a long time since you paid us a visit, marshal. You know you're always more than welcome at the Double C.'

Stewart nodded and turned towards Herne: 'This here's Jed Herne. He's my new deputy, like you said. Some of your boys took care of the old one.'

She gave him a look that would have had a lot of men scuttling for the door, then offered Herne her hand.

'Jed,' said Stewart, 'this is Bathsheba Emerson. The Double C is all hers.'

Her hand on Jed's was as soft as a snake about to strike.

She stepped back, Herne forgotten, her green eyes appraising Dan Stewart. 'Come and sit down. Have some coffee.'

'We don't have the time, there's . . .'

'Nonsense. I had the cook see to it when you first rode into sight.'

And with that she turned and walked into the room by the foot of the stairs, leaving the white door open behind her. Stewart and Herne exchanged glances, then followed her.

The room was furnished to a standard of comfort that Herne had rarely seen away from the east or New Orleans.

Deep comfortable armchairs, a long sofa stacked with a number of brightly coloured cushions; tables with more bowls of flowers and strange ornaments; a large fireplace with logs heaped beside an empty wrought iron grate; above this a portrait in oils of Bathsheba Emerson herself.

Apart from the painting, Herne thought, what the room reminded him most of was one of the better New Orleans brothels.

'A dime for your thoughts, Mister Herne.'

Jed looked at her and shook his head slowly, fearing that he was blushing under her gaze. 'No, ma'am.'

'I'm surprised, Mister Herne, I didn't take you for a bashful man. That wasn't the report my men brought back to me.'

The door opened and a coloured maid came in with a tray. She put it down on the table closest to her mistress and walked back out. It was the first time Herne had seen a black servant so far north west. Again, he glanced at Bathsheba and again he wondered about her. But the lady's eyes were once more firmly fixed on Dan Stewart's handsome face.

'Black or white, gentlemen?' she asked, rising. The coffee was poured from a tall pot that looked to be made of silver. Her hands and arms moved over it like ivory. She was, Herne thought, the best preserved woman of some forty years that he'd encountered.

'Now then, marshal,' she said when they were all sitting again, 'you wanted to talk to me about something.'

Stewart set his cup and saucer on the floor. 'You know about last night, of course. I don't know how that ramrod of yours told it, but . . .'

Bathsheba held up a hand: 'He said that foolish kid talked out of turn and suffered for it. He laid no blame on you, Mister Herne, none at all.'

'He didn't tell you they all bust in there lookin' fer a fight?'

'Why, Mister Herne, I'm sure my men wouldn't do any such thing.'

Herne sat back and said nothing. Stewart was less hesitant. 'That won't wear, Miss Emerson. Not after what Tolly and those other men of yours got involved in.'

'Tolly was always wild, marshal. You know that. I should have fired him a long time ago. He was only allowed into town because Shay Brennan was going along. I thought he could handle Tolly. I'm sorry about that.'

Stewart stood up. 'So are a few new widows an' orphans.'

'What about Shay Brennan's kinfolk?' she blazed back at him. 'And the others your man killed. What about them?'

Stewart turned and walked over to the window; Herne sat where he was admiring the fire in the woman's eyes. There was something in her fierce anger that made it less absurd that she should be the owner of a place like the Double C. There was also a lot about her that made Herne more than usually curious.

For a while none of the three spoke: voices drifted into the house from the corral.

'You surely didn't ride all the way out from town to lose your temper, marshal.'

Bathsheba Emerson moved towards the window, stopping only when she was close enough to have touched Dan Stewart with her hand. When he faced her, his manner was only slightly less hostile.

'I've come to say two things. One concerns Tolly. It's a week before the circuit judge gets to Liberation. In that time I aim to see that he stays where he is and any attempt by your men to get him out of my jail will get them either shut up with him or shot down. The other concerns Jed there—what he did agin Shay an' the others he was doin' as part of his job. He'd bin properly deputised an' they got what they asked for. So I want no more of your boys ridin' into town to pick a fight with him an' get their own back on Tolly's account. On your account, maybe.'

She took a pace past him and stood close to the glass of the window. The light shone on the edges of her hair. Once again, Herne caught himself thinking what a truly handsome woman she was.

'I don't care anything for Tolly, marshal. Like I said, he was wild and likely got what he deserved. I'm sorry about the others but I'm not about to wage a vendetta against the town on their account. Of that I assure you.' She moved gracefully to the centre of the room. 'When my men next come into town it won't be to make trouble for your deputy or to try and break Tolly out of your jail.'

'Do I have your word on that?' Stewart asked.

'My hand, marshal. You may have my hand on it.'

Dan Stewart ignored the offered hand. 'Your word will do, Miss Emerson. And understand, if it's broken then you're the one I shall hold responsible.'

Bathsheba lowered her eyes for a moment. 'I understand you, marshal.'

Stewart thanked her for the coffee and he and Herne moved towards the door. When they were across the hall and Stewart was collecting his hat, she spoke again: 'Drop by again, marshal. And next time, don't feel compelled to bring a bodyguard.'

Dan Stewart jammed his hat into place and pushed open the front door. He was down the steps well ahead of Herne and heading for his horse fast. Herne followed more slowly, wondering why he was rushing away from such an attractive woman with such speed.

Maybe he just didn't like to mix business with pleasure.

Neither man said much as they began their ride back to town, each apparently lost in his own thoughts.

The sky had begun to cloud over and a wind had got up, driving down the valley towards them. Herne stopped and freed his coat from the straps behind his saddle. The grass that sloped up from the path wavered like a green sea.

'That sure is some woman,' Herne said when he had drawn level with Stewart again.

The marshal looked at him and nodded in agreement.

'How come you didn't tell me we was goin' to see a woman?'

Stewart smiled: 'Thought you'd figure that out for yourself soon enough.'

'How long she bin bossin' the Double C?'

'Since before I came here. Well before. Ten or more years, I guess.'

'Know anything about her before that?'

Stewart took his time before answering. 'Rumours. That's all. Ain't worth tradin' in rumours nohow.'

Herne thought from the tone of Dan Stewart's voice and the changed expression on his face that he likely knew what he was talking about. His mind went back to the unanswered question about why the young marshal had left Ogden. Then he looked ahead and the wind struck at his face and blew the thoughts from his mind.

'Reckon she'll keep her word?' Herne asked when they were nearer Liberation.

'Long as it suits her.'

'You don't sound as if you trust her, Dan.'

'I'll tell you, Jed, I don't trust any woman. Not nohow.'

'Well, she sure acts sweet on you. There's got to be something in that.'

Dan Stewart nodded and set his face: 'Damn right, Jed. Just one thing . . .'

'Go ahead.'

'Trouble.'

Herne would have liked to ask more, but he sensed it was the wrong time. He dropped back a few yards and gazed at the outline of the hills on either side, darker now and misted at the tops. The sky sat heavily on them, a dull slate grey.

'Rider comin', Jed!'

Herne had seen him, though a few seconds after Stewart, who already had his rifle in his right hand and had pulled his horse to the right of the track. Herne freed his .55 Sharps and went to the left. Whoever it was didn't care too much about running his mount into the ground; whatever his reasons for riding like that they had to be pretty damned important.

Forty yards away from the two lawmen, the rider started to slow down and Stewart put up his weapon.

'It's young Radley. Helps out at the livery stable.'

Herne kept his own rifle at the ready and waited.

'Marshal Stewart! Marshal Stewart!'

The youngster reined in his horse, both of them lathered with sweat. He jumped down from the saddle, almost losing his balance.

'Take it easy, Radley. What's the all-fired hurry?'

'It's Tolly, Marshal. Tolly!'

'What about him?'

'He's gone.'

'Gone! What in hell's name you talkin' about?'

The boy coughed and stumbled over his words, breathing roughly. 'They . . . he . . . they come and bust him out. Smashed the jail plumb open. They . . .'

Stewart got down and went towards him. 'All right, easy now. Who're this "they" you keep on about?'

'Don't rightly know. Didn't see 'em myself. Maybe a dozen men. They came roarin' into town, shootin, an . . .'

Stewart put his hand on Radley's shoulder. 'I thought you said you didn't see 'em.'

'Well, no, but that's what folks are sayin'.'

'Never mind that,' Herne put in. 'Stick to the facts.'

The boy looked up at Herne: 'Fact is, mister, they bust Tolly from the jail and rode off out of town with him. Guess that's the only fact I know for sure.'

'An' that's the one we want. You did well, son.'

'Sure,' added Stewart, giving the kid a friendly slap on the back. 'You done well to ride out for us.'

The youngster blushed deep red and smiled in spite of himself. A broken-toothed grin under freckled cheeks. 'Thanks, Marshal. Thanks.' He looked at the two lawmen expectantly. 'You goin' t' ride like all hell into town and chase after 'em?'

Stewart shook his head. 'No point in that, son. If Tolly's gone, he's gone. No amount of racin' around's goin' to alter that.'

'But . . .'

'No sense in breakin' an animal for no good reason.'

'But . . .'

'Damn it, Radley, you're gettin' to sound like one of them telegraph machines, buttin' an' stutterin' all the time. You take that horse of yorn down to the stream and let her water an' rest up a while before you come back.'

'But . . .'

'Jesus, Radley, quit that an' do as I say. You done a good job already. Don't go spoilin' it.'

'No, sir. An' thank you, sir.'

Radley started to walk his mount down to the stream, looking over his shoulder all the time at the two lawmen as they rode slow and easy back to town.

'What d'you reckon, Dan?' asked Herne.

'Can't say. Don't see how it could've been the Double C. An' I don't figure anyone else wantin' to bust Tolly loose. Guess we'll have to wait an' see.'

Herne set his face into the wind: the marshal was right —it was all that they could do. For now.

CHAPTER EIGHT

There was still a crowd of townspeople around the front of the marshal's office. Men who didn't have any work to do, women and small kids, a handful of down-and-outs who hoped someone would get excited enough by what had happened to toss them a few cents for beer. The crowd began to separate as soon as the two lawmen appeared at the end of the street, making a channel through which Herne and Stewart could ride.

As the two men got nearer, Quentin Faulkner began to hurry across the street from The Cattlemen's House, anger showing clearly in his face and the determination of his stride. The burly shape of Wilbur Merz appeared at the far side of the crowd, hands resting over the slope of his belly.

'See here, marshal, what right had both you and your deputy to be riding out of town and leaving your prisoner unguarded? I demand . . .'

Stewart gave Faulkner little more than a glance. 'Demand away, Faulkner. It ain't goin' t' get you anywhere.'

'It is my belief,' the owner of The Cattlemen's House shouted at their backs as they passed beyond him, 'that you left town with the specific purpose of allowing your friends at the Double C to ride in and take that Tolly to freedom.'

Herne saw Stewart flinch: a wave of amazement and surprise ran through the crowd. Dan Stewart turned in his saddle and looked at Faulkner as though he were nothing more than dog vomit.

'Tell you what to do with your beliefs, Faulkner. You can choke on 'em till you drown.'

Faulkner's face blazed. 'Look, marshal, I'd best remind you that I'm the head of the town council and you cannot talk to me in that manner.'

Stewart swung his horse round. 'An' I'll remind you that I'm marshal here in town an' it ain't for you to tell me how to do my job.'

'I don't call giving the Double C a free hand . . .'

'Who in hell's name says it was the Double C? You see 'em Faulkner?'

Faulkner waved a podgy hand in Stewart's direction. 'I didn't have to see them to know. Who else would want to free that gunman but those friends of yours?'

Stewart's fingers tightened about the saddle pommel. 'Careful what you're sayin' about the Double C bein' my friends.'

Faulkner allowed himself a smile. 'Come now, marshal, do you deny that's where you have just returned from? Why the whole town knows about you and that Emerson woman.'

There was a blur of movement and the Remington that was holstered on Stewart's chest had been pulled clear in the fastest cross-draw that Herne had ever witnessed.

Faulkner stammered, stuttered, went white. His arms fell to his sides. 'Don't . . . you can't . . . you . . .'

'Damn you, you snivellin' bastard! You take back what you just said!'

'I didn't . . .'

Stewart eased back the hammer of the gun.

'No, please. Please!'

'Get down on your knees and take back what you said!'

Quentin Faulkner stared around the crowd, open-mouthed and desperate for some sign of assistance. But folk either looked away or stared back at him with obvious relish. When his eyes met those of Wilbur Merz, the banker's glazed over as if his fellow councillor wasn't even there.

'Please!'

'Get down, you lyin' bastard!'

The gun moved an inch; Faulkner closed his eyes and, tears almost bursting from his face, he knelt in the dirt of the street in front of a crowd of drunks and hangers-on, women and fool kids. His head was bent low so that no one could see the humiliation pictured there.

'Now say you lied.'

Faulkner's body shook, but no words came.

'Say it!'

The crowd was totally silent.

'I . . . I didn't know what . . . what I was saying about . . . about the marshal and the Double C . . .'

'Or Miss Emerson.'

'Or Miss Emerson.'

Faulkner's head went all the way forward, till the ends of his hair were touching the dirt. People at the back of the crowd began to snigger, then one or two laughed outright. Wilbur Merz turned his back and walked slowly towards the bank.

As the noise from the crowd rose to a crescendo, Stewart released the hammer of his gun and slid it back into its holster. Herne dismounted and tied up his horse, then stepped onto the boardwalk.

'Get away!' he ordered the crowd. 'Get on with your business. Whatever there was to see, you seen it.'

He walked through the open door into the office, Stewart following him a few moments later. The desk had been pushed up against the side wall and a couple of chairs turned over; generally the place looked a mess. But that hadn't been what the men were interested in.

The door that led through to the cells had been ripped off its hinges and lay back against the wall, smashed beyond repair. Inside, the lock to Tolly's cell had been shot away; the iron-barred door was half open. Whoever it had been had come in force.

'We'd best be movin'.' Stewart started to take boxes of cartridges from the wall cupboard.

'Know where to?'

'No. But with that many it shouldn't be hard to pick up their trail.'

Herne took some .45 shells for his own gun. 'Guess they'll know that sure enough.'

'Right. They'll either split up or else send someone back to watch for us—that's the way I see it. You?'

Herne looked up. 'Sounds reasonable. Only way we're goin' to catch up with Tolly is by trackin' 'em down, though.'

'Surely is. Let's go.'

As the two men rode out of town, the crumpled shape of Quentin Faulkner sat hunched in the privacy of his office. Two lines ran down his face where the tears he'd been unable to stop had coursed through the caking of dust that had risen up from the street. The knees of his suit were marked with dirt. He sat there, alone, trying to wipe the memory of it from his mind, knowing that it would not be easy.

The trousers he could brush, his face he could wash—but his mind. There would be only one way to bury his humiliation—and that would mean burying Dan Stewart as well.

'Trail breaks off here, Dan.'

Herne pointed down to a mess of hoofprints on the ground. 'Small group of 'em fork off south, rest stay west.'

'Well, wherever they're headin', it sure ain't the Double C.'

'No, but if it was them, they wouldn't be likely to lead us straight back to the ranch.'

The two men rode on cautiously, anticipating an ambush. The slate sky had cracked apart and the sun spilled its warmth over them as they travelled. To the west aspens quivered in the breeze; out of sight beyond the hills to the east came the sound of lowing cattle in the mid-distance.

Once Herne stopped short at a movement in the trees, his Sharps pulled clear, but it was only a large, black bird.

And still the tracks of the larger of the two groups headed forwards; whoever it was had made no attempt to cover their path. Half a mile further on, Herne and Stewart found out why.

The tree was on a crest that pushed up against the skyline; the middle one of three. Their branches all pointed towards the east, set by winters of wind. From the strongest branch of the tree, Tolly's body twisted slowly, a rocking movement, side to side.

'Well, I'll be . . .'

'Now that's somethin' I guess we neither of us figured.'

'Sure answers a few questions, Jed.'

'Guess it does. Asks a whole lot more, though. Let's get to it.'

They set their horses to a trot and crossed the open stretch of plain that led up to the three trees, both men grim-faced and thinking their own thoughts.

Tolly's arms had been secured behind him and his legs had been tied fast at both ankles and knees. It was a tall branch and impossible to hang a man from his saddle. They would somehow have had to have made Tolly stand on his horse instead of sitting on it—then whipped it away.

The thick cord of rope about his neck had burnt through the skin and a double necklace of blood shone above and beneath it. The head lolled to one side, purple tongue pushing between darkened lips. Yet Tolly's face looked younger than Herne remembered it, more peaceful. For all the world like a kid who'd been out picking blueberries and eating them.

Except for the angle of the neck.

Except for the mass of flies that swarmed around the seat and legs of his pants where he'd shat himself in the moment of dying.

Dan Stewart climbed the trunk and shinned along the branch until he was within reach of the rope. He sliced through it with his knife and Jed caught the body as it fell, laying it out on the ground.

'Jesus! One of us's got to take this stinkin' thing back to town.'

'Hate to say it, Jed, but you're the deputy.'

Herne grinned ruefully. 'Yep, but like you said the other day, you pull a lot more money than I do. You got to do somethin' extra to earn all that.'

Dan Stewart made a face, but he picked up the stiffening body nonetheless and draped it over his horse, tying it down with rope.

'Boy,' said Herne, 'am I goin' to ride well downwind of you!'

The two lawmen stood in the middle of Liberation's main street. Tolly had been deposited with the local undertaker and the crowd that had gathered to watch his return to town had dispersed just as quickly.

'Jesus! I need a drink after that. Ain't seen too many hanged men close up that it don't get to my gut.'

Herne, who had seen a good many killed by hanging and worse, looked at the younger man and said nothing.

'Only thing is, with you unpopular at The Five Aces an' me at The Cattlemen's House, we're runnin' out of places to buy us a beer.'

Herne grinned: 'Never did know a lawman any good at his job who was popular with very many folk—specially them he was hired to protect. 'Sides, you ain't afraid of Faulkner, are you?'

For an answer, Stewart set off towards The Cattlemen's House. He ordered a beer for himself and a bourbon for Herne and pushed a way through the idlers and gawpers who were chewing tobacco and discussing young Tolly's lynching.

'What you goin' t' do 'bout it, marshal?'

'Yep, marshal, you goin' t' catch them lynchin' bastards?'

'Marshal?'

Stewart sat in one of the booths near the stairs and Herne sat opposite him, drinking and waiting for the demands of the men round the bar to die down.

Josie came bustling out of the kitchen and gave Herne a wave and a bright smile.

'Hey, Josie!'

'What can I do for you, Mister Herne?'

'Jed.'

'Jed, then.'

'I could use a steak and eggs. How 'bout you, Dan?'

Stewart made a face and shook his head.

'Now, marshal,' joked Josie, 'you know my cooking ain't that bad.' She hurried off back to the kitchen.

Stewart looked at him. 'That why you took a room down the street, 'stead of usin' the one by the jail?'

Herne sat forward, elbows on the table: 'Maybe it is an' maybe it ain't. One thing, though, whatever the reason, it's sure my business an' nobody else's. You may have good reasons for your feelin's 'bout women, but they ain't got nothin' to do with me.'

'Hey, steady on, Jed. I didn't mean nothin' by it. Josie's nice enough—for a woman.'

'Huh!' Herne sat back and swallowed his bourbon. The door to Faulkner's office opened a little then shut fast. Round the bar folk were still busily talking about what had happened to Tolly.

Herne waited till he was half way through his steak before he asked Dan the same question most other folks in town were asking.

'I don't rightly know who done it. Whoever it was split up the other side of that hangin' tree an' we'd be fools to try an' track all of 'em. Course, I got a few ideas, but ideas don't prove nothin'.'

'That's right, but I'd like to hear 'em just the same.'

Stewart sank the last of his beer and wiped his hand round his brown moustache. 'There's . . .'

He didn't get any further. There was a shout from out in the street and a whole lot of commotion down at the bar. The name 'Emerson' drifted through the welter of noise and then there she was standing in the doorway.

She was wearing black this time, the cloth smeared and stained with the dirt of a hard, fast ride. Her dark hair was pushed up underneath a fawn hat and she wore a gun belt with a curved-handled Smith and Wesson .32 in the holster. Her green eyes were blazing with more fury than Herne had even seen in one woman.

Nor was she alone.

Scott Miller was right behind her, whip and pistol in their usual places, anger showing in his face also. There were other Double C men just through the doors on the boardwalk.

The saloon was silent.

'Marshal Stewart!'

The woman's voice rang through the large room like a bell tolling the end of the world.

Dan Stewart stood away from the booth, moving slow, not wanting to start anything before he knew what he was into.

'Miss Emerson.'

'We brought you something, marshal.'

She flicked her hand at Miller, who turned to one side and called a couple of his men forward. They walked into the saloon and a gasp went up from everyone round the bar.

They were carrying one of the cowboys between them,

holding an arm and a leg each. They moved him head first, so that the head itself fell forward and stared up at Stewart with eyes that were open and dead. The man's mouth was open, too, and below another, wider mouth yawned where his throat had been cut. The bubbles of blood that had sprung from it had dried into crimson lips.

'Set him down, boys.'

The Double C men laid the dead cowboy out on one of the tables, head and legs falling over the edges. Bathsheba Emerson stepped up alongside the body and pointed at it.

'Recognise him, marshal? Curly Young, one of my best punchers. Been with me for five years. A good man, steady, not a drinker, never drew down on another man in his whole life. A law abiding citizen of this territory, marshal—the sort of a man you and your friend there are paid to protect.'

Mumbling from the drinkers, sounds of shuffling, awkward feet. Herne could see more people gathering outside. He cut off a chunk of steak and set it to his mouth. No point in letting good food go cold.

'Don't you want to know what happened to him, marshal? You don't seem awful curious, standing up there like that. Perhaps you know already.' She stared at him accusingly. 'But in case you don't, I'll tell you. Curly was out riding line, him and one of the other boys. Some dozen of them came up fast. Rode them down. Mitch got away but, as you can see, Curly wasn't so lucky. They cut his throat and brought him near enough to the ranch house for us to see him. There was a note on his body, just so that we'd know who'd done it.'

Bathsheba Emerson ran the tip of her tongue round her lips; they were dry and the back of her mouth felt parched.

Dan Stewart said his first word for some time: 'Who?'

She took a pace towards him, then another. 'You mean you don't know, marshal? You don't know who did this to one of my boys?'

'If'n I knew, ma'am, I wouldn't be wasting my breath asking.'

Herne watched closely, wiping a piece of bread round his plate and pushing it into his mouth.

'It was the Broken Bar, marshal. Who else did you think it could be? Hastings and the Broken Bar.'

Everyone started talking at once; almost everyone. Herne and Stewart exchanged hasty glances.

'You say Hastings was there?'

'Of course he wasn't. He wouldn't do his own dirty work when he can pay others to do it for him. But it was his men, right enough.'

Stewart started to walk down the saloon. Fifteen yards away from her he stopped. 'You brought the note?' he asked, left hand outstretched.

Bathsheba Emerson reached behind her and Miller put the note into her hand. She unfolded it and read it aloud: *'This is a warning. Every time my stock is rustled by you thieves from the Double C, your men will pay the bill. It's time someone took care of the law round here and we're going to do it—like we did with that murderer Tolly.'*

Stewart continued on his way. Herne had moved from the booth and was covering the marshal from an angle to the left, watching Scott Miller and the men behind him. Stewart took the note from Bathsheba Emerson's hand and read it slowly twice. Then he folded it up and pushed it into his back pocket.

'What you aimin' to do, Miss Emerson?'

'What do you think?' Her voice was like a slap.

'I hope you're goin' to take Curly back to the ranch and bury him proper. Nothin' more.'

Bathsheba threw back her head and laughed, a sharp ringing laugh that echoed round the saloon. When she spoke it was almost in a whisper. 'We'll take Curly back home all right. Then we're going to mount up and ride over to the Broken Bar and show Hastings what kind of trouble he's bought.'

'No, you ain't.'

She laughed again, full in the marshal's face, and started to turn away from him. He grabbed at her arm and as he did so Scott Miller went for his gun.

'Freeze!'

Jed Herne had seen the move and his own had been faster. The ramrod's pistol was half-way out of his holster when Herne's Colt was drawn and pointing at him, hammer cocked back. The big man snarled and let the gun slide back into his holster.

'Any of you make a move an' you're dead men!'

The Double C boys looked at Herne's gun and believed him. No one made another play. Stewart still had Bathsheba Emerson's arm tight within his hand and she stood her ground, green eyes glaring hatred at him.

'Let me go!'

Stewart shook his head and she tried to pull away from him; he held fast and she aimed a slap at his face with her free hand but he parried the blow and then beat her to the .32 at her hip. Stewart tossed the little gun back along the floor towards where Herne was standing, covering the rest of the Double C gang.

'Don't you dare!'

She made to slap Stewart again and this time his left hand went fast for the Remington at his chest. The open palm cracked across the marshal's face exactly as the end of the gun barrel pressed home between her breasts.

'Don't!'

She stared at his handsome, angry face with the white marks of her fingers imprinted on his cheek; felt the prodding of his gun in the cleft of her breasts.

'You bein' a woman won't make it any less likely for me to kill you.'

She wrenched her arm free and he took half a pace

back. 'What I hear,' she hissed, 'it's all the more likely, not less.'

Miller glared at Stewart: 'I'm goin' to tell you something, marshal. Next time we meet up you'd best go for one of them guns of yours right off. 'Cause I ain't goin' to let no man treat Miss Emerson that way. Not an' live.'

'Stop runnin' off at the mouth, Miller,' snapped Herne, 'or I'll put a bullet in you right now.'

Stewart fished out the note and held it in his hand, showing it to Bathsheba. 'I want your word you'll let us handle this.'

'You're joking . . .'

'I ain't. You take your men back to the Double C and wait.'

'For what, marshal? An invitation to your funeral?'

'Maybe. That's my affair. But you're going back—this is law business. Like you said yourself.'

'And if I refuse?'

'You and your boys can spend the night here in jail.'

Bathsheba stamped her foot in temper and slapped a hand against her thigh. 'Damn you, marshal! Damn you!' She rounded on her heel and pushed through her men and out into the street.

Herne moved after her, herding Miller and the rest of Double C boys onto their horses.

'Want me to ride with 'em a-ways, Dan?' he asked.

Stewart shook his head. 'Miss Emerson knows what's right by the law. She'll go back to the ranch for today. Won't you, ma'am?'

The woman hissed an inaudible reply through her teeth and jerked at her horse's rein, pulling it away and into the street. She tossed her head and the hat fell backwards, revealing her pinned-up hair.

'You've got till this time tomorrow, marshal. You and your . . . your friend there. After that this town will see that Hastings isn't the only one to take the law into his own hands!'

With a whirl of dust, she galloped out of town, her men following, the dead body of Curly Young bouncing on the back of the spare horse to which it was tied.

CHAPTER NINE

It hadn't been easy for Herne to talk Dan Stewart into letting him ride out alone to the Broken Bar. But finally Herne had persuaded him that if the two of them rode in there together it was likely to lead to shooting before many words got spoken. Besides, Herne didn't trust some of the Double C boys not to come back into town and stir up things there.

So the two lawmen split up, with Stewart staying in Liberation and Herne riding out towards the North Platte River.

At the edge of Broken Bar territory he came upon wire, stretched out in both directions for as far as the eye could see. A little way in and he could see the sails of the wind pump turning gently in the breeze. And then the sound of hoofs and a dust that clouded the new brightness of the day.

Herne's hand automatically went to his Colt; his left hand slid the Sharps a few inches from its place by the saddle. He reined in his horse and waited.

Likely they'd see who he was and what he wanted before they started going for their guns.

Likely . . .

If they didn't . . .

There were four of them and as soon as they saw him they split up, still heading in his direction but letting fifteen to twenty yards of daylight separate them, making it more difficult for one man to pick them off.

Whoever had taught them their business, thought Herne, had done it pretty well.

When they saw Herne was making no attempt to go for a gun or to ride off, the centre pair pulled back together again, coming directly for him, the others standing off.

'What's your business, mister?'

'Look at that badge he got on him, Seth.'

The man named Seth drew back his head and stared at Herne's chest, then let his right hand get awful close to his gun butt. Herne narrowed his eyes, let the cowboy see that he'd noticed the move, but let it go.

'I said, what's your business, mister?'

'You seen the badge,' said Herne. 'Ain't that enough?'

'Not out here it ain't. This is Broken Bar range. This ain't town.'

'Don't you have no law out here?'

Seth tapped his Colt: 'This.'

'And Hastings?' Herne asked.

The man alongside Seth grinned. 'It's his ranch. His word what calls the tune.'

'He says what's law and what ain't,' said Herne. 'That it?'

'You ask a lot of questions, marshal.'

'What I'm paid fer.'

'An' that gun you're wearin'—you paid to use that, too?'

'What d'you think?'

'I think someone might be payin' you too much.'

'I wouldn't lay bets if I was you.'

Seth sneered and left his hand on the butt of his pistol.

Herne let his horse move a little under him. He reckoned the two on the flanks weren't up to much and could probably be discounted. Seth was getting itchy with that trigger finger of his, just dying to squeeze back on the Colt he was wearing. The one with him didn't seem so keen for gunplay, but he wore his gun strapped to his leg like he knew how to use it.

'We're wastin' time, Seth.'

'You're right.' He came a mite nearer to Herne. 'You was tellin' us your business on Broken Bar land.'

'I weren't, but I'm here to see Hastings.'

'On whose say-so?'

For answer, Herne tapped the badge that was reflecting the sun in tiny shafts of light.

'Mister, I told you what we think of the law here!'

'Seth, for ...'

'Jesus!'

Herne had gone for his gun when neither man before him had expected it and his speed had been impossible for them to follow. All they knew was that they were suddenly staring, not at the man with greying hair, but at the end of his Colt .45.

'Let that hand of yorn drift away from your gun belt. Do it easy now.'

'Hell, I ...'

'Do it, Seth.'

One more glance at Herne's face and Seth took his friend's advice.

'You two out there, ride in where I can see you better. And keep both hands well clear of anything that might get you into trouble.'

They rode over, worry under their stetsons, ordinary cowpunchers who were none too keen on getting involved in a fight—especially when the chances of coming out on top didn't look so good. He was only one man, but ... but he'd got the drop on Seth and Montana like they never saw him move.

'Okay, now we'll all take us a ride down to Mister Hastings. Me behind and you four in front.' Herne let them see the gun in his hand clearly. 'Any one of you decides to be a hero, he's goin' to earn himself a quick, cheap funeral. That understood?'

Nods and grunts.
'Then let's get goin'.'

The Broken Bar didn't have the style of the Double C, not when it came to the main ranch house. But it did seem bigger and more solid: like Hastings had had it built to stay. Stay and grow.

There was only one other Broken Bar man in sight as Herne rode in—an old timer nailing pieces of fresh planking onto one of the outhouses. He turned his head slowly as the riders approached, then jerked fully round, almost choking on the nail he held between toothless gums. Finally his mouth dropped open and the nail fell to the ground.

What in tarnation was going on? Seth and Montana and a couple of the other boys being ridden herd on by one man.

The old man blinked and saw the badge on Herne's shirt as the big man rode closer. He reached for the hammer and stood with it in his hand as the procession passed him by.

They were close to the ranch house, when the door opened and Clifford Hastings made his appearance. Herne wondered from how far off he had seen them coming.

He had on a black suit, though Herne was sweating under the shirt he wore and the day looked to get a whole lot hotter before it cooled down. A watch chain dangled from his waistcoat; the long fingers hung patiently by his sides.

Herne could see no sign of a gun, but didn't doubt that the rancher wore one somewhere.

'Marshal,' he said in greeting. 'I see you stayed in the job longer than you figured when we were talking.'

'Seems like.'

Hastings took another pace forward. 'If I didn't know better, I'd think you was arresting my men there. That's the way it looks.'

Herne shook his head: 'Ain't arresting anybody yet. Just come in to talk.' He nodded in the cowboys' direction. 'They didn't see it that way.'

Hastings smiled and gestured with one hand. 'Don't reckon too much to that, marshal, I guess they might have been a little hasty, but that's understandable. Considering . . .'

'Considering what?'

'Trouble we're having with the Double C.'

Herne's face broke into a broad smile. 'You got gall, Hastings, I'll give you that much.'

'Marshal Herne, I don't . . .'

'Like hell you don't!'

Hastings looked closely up at Herne: he wasn't smiling any longer. 'Let's step inside and talk about this. What d'you say?'

Herne nodded: 'That's what I rode out this way for.'

Hastings had a quick word with Montana, telling him to get the others back out onto the range double quick. Then he showed Herne into the house.

It was very different from the Emerson place. The furniture was rough and heavy, a thick layer of dust clouded the surfaces, shown up by the sunlight that filtered through windows patterned with months of dirt. The rug on the floor of the room where Hastings led him was worn and patched. There was a musty smell, as if the room hadn't been aired for ages.

'You aren't averse to a drink?'

'I'll take some whisky.'

Hastings got up: 'Jack Daniels suit you?'

'Fine.'

Herne watched, fascinated, as the long, spidery fingers picked up the square-shaped bottle and poured some of the contents into two glasses.

'What are we drinking to?' Hastings asked, holding his own glass high.

'Law and order?' Herne suggested, challengingly.

Hastings didn't hesitate, but put back his head and drank.

'What d'you think of the ranch?'

'Didn't see too much, but what I seen, it's fine. Good grazing land. Plenty of water. Guess you'll be driving a pretty big herd down to Cheyenne in a few weeks?'

Hastings stood up and walked towards the window at the end of the room. When he turned to face Herne again, his hands were in front of him, palms apart, tips of the fingers together to form an arch. He gazed down at the shape for several seconds before speaking again.

'You're right. It is good land. It is a big ranch. But . . . ?'

'But it could be bigger.'

'Correct. Without the Double C.'

'This country's big enough fer you both to grow as much as you like.'

'No.' Hastings separated his hands, walked back towards his chair; stood with his arms resting on its back. 'For one thing, the way to expand is with the line of the river—and their land's in the way. For another, they've been harrying and rustling my stock for the best part of a year.'

'You say.'

Hastings brown eyes flickered dangerously. 'That wouldn't be calling me a liar?'

'It'd be sayin' that Dan Stewart's sweated a lot of time trackin' down so-called rustlers from the Double C an' ain't come up with a thing.'

'And you take his word against mine?'

Herne set down his glass slowly and deliberately, then stood up. 'Yes. Yes, I do.'

'Even allowing for what's between Stewart and that Emerson woman?'

'Which is nothing—at least, not as far as Dan Stewart is concerned, it ain't.'

Hastings straightened up, took out his watch and looked

at it, then replaced it at the front of his waiscoat.

'Expecting company?'

'No.'

'Tired of talkin', maybe.'

'Not at all.'

'How 'bout this then? If you get enough stories goin' 'bout the Double C rustling your stock an' the law don't do nothin' about it—on account of the fact it ain't really happenin'—no one's goin' to blame you fer taking matters into your own hands. Like that business with Curly Young. An' with Tolly.'

Hastings managed to look surprised. 'What business? I heard something about Tolly being sprung from jail, but...'

Herne stepped towards the ranch owner. 'Tolly was sprung all right. Sprung from the neck. Right after that one of the Double C boys had his throat cut.'

'And what makes you think it was Broken Bar work?'

Herne took the crumpled note from his pants and gave it to Hastings, who read it quickly before dropping it onto the seat of the chair.

'It's a fool trick to lay blame on us.'

'They'd kill two of their own men to do that?'

'Bathsheba Emerson would do anything to see me and my ranch wiped off the face of the earth. Anything! You don't understand her cunning or her determination. You can't.'

'What about her motives, Hastings? Why should she want rid of you so bad?'

The rancher looked as if he was about to answer, but turned away instead.

'I could make a guess,' offered Herne. 'Two people, powerful, man an' a woman. Nothin' more natural than that they should meet, become attracted, arrange to marry maybe.'

He could tell by the high flush on Hastings' cheekbones that he had struck at something near to the truth.

'Which of you broke it off, Hastings? Who's got the biggest reason to hate?'

Hastings stretched his hands, cracked the knuckles of first the left, then the right. 'I think you've outstayed your welcome, Marshal.'

'You orderin' me off?'

'Advising.'

'All right. But before I go make sure you understand one thing—there's only one law in this territory and it ain't your law. Nor the Double C's. Vigilantes an' lynchin' parties an' the like, they're worse than whatever they're aimin' to cut down. You hold that tight in your mind an' think on it before anythin' else happens.'

Herne stood by the door, letting Hastings see his right hand hover close to his Colt. 'I don't want to come back here usin' this, Hastings, but if I have to, I will. I'm a man as does what he's paid for—an' right now that's keepin' the law in these parts. Don't you forget it.'

From the window Clifford Hastings watched Herne go, a tall figure walking to his horse, mounting up and riding casually away from the ranch house. Hastings wasn't one to underestimate a man—and he'd seen what Herne could do with a gun that first night in Liberation.

Yes, if Herne came back there after him it would mean a lot of trouble. But that was a big word ... that 'if'. He took out his watch again and looked at the time, making calculations in his head.

Damn Herne and his impudence, talking about Bathsheba and himself like that!

Damn him!

Herne let his horse move at its own pace, trying to figure out how far his warning had gone with Hastings. In the end, he decided not very far at all. When a ranch owner got that big there was only one thing most of them wanted—and that was to get bigger still. It was one thing to own a small spread of your own—like the one he and Louise had worked and grown to know and care for—

but another to own thousands of acres, hundreds of head of cattle. To have that much power over man and beast: that much wealth.

No: Clifford Hastings wouldn't be content to stick with what he had. Especially with the Double C standing in his way ... for the Double C was Bathsheba Emerson. Herne had hit home on a nerve there right enough.

Raw nerve.

He wondered what state their relationship had been in when Dan Stewart had come along to be marshal. What difference Bathsheba's feelings for him had made?

A feud between two people who were neither of them likely to back down this side of dying. A feud with Dan Stewart in the middle and himself alongside him—now that he'd taken the badge to wear and a few paltry dollars for his pay.

How had Stewart described it when he'd asked Herne to take the job? About to burst open and explode? Well, that was sure enough right. It surely ...

He saw the man almost before the shell whipped past his head; felt the wind of it almost before he heard the shot. Herne glanced quickly round in search of cover that didn't exist. He was in the middle of open range and they knew it—had wanted it like that.

He pulled at his horse's rein, touching its flanks with his spurs and calling to it as he bent low over its neck and started into a gallop that would take him away from the group of riders that was coming up behind. Away from them and off at an angle from the man who'd tried to drop him from the saddle with a rifle.

Power of the animal beneath him surged up through his thighs as he felt it straining for distance; shots sang out but Herne ignored them, knowing that his pursuers were coming at him with speed and only a lucky shot would hit home.

And if his luck was out, well, there was nothing he could do about that.

Ahead of him the land swung into a gradual rise where it followed the contours that would eventually bring it up to the hills in the distance.

Herne felt the sun on his back, on the back of his neck; glanced round again.

To the right there were five riders, to the left and further off, three more. He couldn't recognise any of them travelling at that speed but he guessed that Seth and Montana were among them.

So much for Hastings: he'd planned this little show even before hearing what Herne had to say.

A couple of shells raked the ground only a couple of feet to his right. He'd make the side of the slope—such as it was—then use the Sharps. Just to get the odds down to size.

The big gun was already out and in his hand when he willed the stallion into a further burst of pace. Time to slow and turn, bring up the rifle and take aim . . .

Herne's first shot smashed into the leading man of the group of five and sent him crashing to the ground. The animal that had been underneath him continued on its way, suddenly free of the weight that had sweated on top of it. After thirty yards it started to move off to the side, cutting across two of the other riders.

By that time Herne had fired twice more. A second Broken Bar cowboy was hanging onto his horse's neck for dear life, while a hole the size of several fingers pulsed blood from the top of his thigh.

A third was dragging from one stirrup; dragging, bouncing, falling clear away, rolling over: still.

Herne had ridden away from the sun, changing position, putting its brightness at the backs of his attackers. Six men now, one of them wounded. He whirled round and drew a bead on the one he could now recognise as Montana. Let the horse slow. Saw Montana's face, chest; up again; fired and the shell tore through the cowboy's neck, leaving a gaping wound where the windpipe had been and exiting at the rear in a stream of blood.

Five.

Before Herne could fire again the wounded man came out of his saddle and sprawled over the ground.

Four.

Herne saw them rein in on their mounts, hesitant about riding towards that big Sharps of his any more. Fine. He rammed it back down under the saddle and called to his horse. Drew his Colt and took off towards them.

One, a skinny youngster with yellowish hair that hung past his shoulders, kept on coming. The others turned and high-tailed it for home.

Herne and the youth drew closer and closer, the sun filling the space behind him, making the ends of his hair gleam until it seemed to be on fire. Herne shaded his eyes, almost didn't see the pistol come up beside the animal's neck. A shot sang out of that bright sun and Herne moved instinctively to one side and brought up his own Colt.

Yellow hair, oh, yellow hair!

As the body jumped and left the horse's back, strands of hair shot up across the roundness of the sun and began to drift back down through it. They were close now and Herne could see the youngster's face as his body fell from the centre of the light and hit the ground. Eyes clenched tight shut. Mouth open.

His back struck the ground and arms and legs arched out, pistol going up into a series of curves and loops, high, high in the air.

Herne reined in and jumped down from his saddle. Colt held ready he walked back to where the youth had fallen. Wanting to be certain; taking care.

He turned him over with his boot. The bullet had taken him in the chest, on the left side and Herne allowed himself a little nod of satisfaction.

Travelling at that speed and against a moving target, it was a shot he could be pleased with. Not so, the Broken Bar cowboy. But at least, thought Herne, he'd had guts;

at least he hadn't turned and run, like Seth and the others.

As Jed Herne walked back to his horse, he felt the warmth of the sun again; his eyes swept over the landscape, over Hastings' land. It was empty of people—except for himself and the youngster with yellow hair. And the youth was dead.

He mounted up and carried on on his way back to town. He had Hastings' answer and it was writ clear: clear in the blood of the men he'd sent out against Herne.

How long would it be, Herne thought, before it had to be written in blood that was Hastings' own?'

CHAPTER TEN

There was enough moonlight coming through the shutters for Herne to be able to pick out the outline of everything in the room—but that wasn't what was keeping him awake. The rail at the foot of the bed; clothes hung from the brass knob at the right hand side; set of drawers; wooden stand with a bowl and jug; chair. No: none of those things.

He was thinking about Clifford Hastings and Bathsheba Emerson: the long, slim fingers of one; the long, dark hair of the other. Sending men out to fight and die for what causes?

Herne's mind went back again to the Lincoln County Range War. A whole territory torn apart by hired guns—guns such as his own. He remembered the excitement, the fresh charge of adrenalin through his body each morning. The men he had fought with or fought against.

But that had been before meeting Louise. Before putting up his gun and getting those hands of his to adapt to the plough and the axe. Calloused they had become, worn and blistered—for the first weeks, his skin had rebelled with blisters the size of dollar pieces. Red and raw when they had burst and the skin had started to form again into another swelling.

It had been worth it for the look on Louise's face when he'd got back to the cabin at the end of the day; a look that had grown in maturity, in confidence since the first time he had laid eyes on her when she'd been no more than sixteen. And him twice her years.

1878.

Six years: and times they seemed like sixty. At others no time at all. He could see her eyes upon him, feel the lightness of her fingers as she traced the lines on his face, felt the strength in his limbs.

Now, when he had no wish to think about her, when he wished she would let him rest, the sight of Louise moved across his mind constantly. A long dress, patterned with flowers. Only close to was it possible to see where it had been stitched up and stitched yet again; where blackberry and apple juice had each left their mark. Herne shook his head but the image persisted. The feel of the body that moved freely beneath that dress. Smell of it. Warm.

'Jed.'

Herne turned and leaned on one arm, looking down at the woman who lay beside him.

'Jed. Why're you awake?'

'It's nothin'.'

'Must be something troubling you.'

Josie came closer to him, shifted her arm against his, her leg coming over one of his own. She reached her face up towards his and, despite himself, he jerked his head backwards.

She frowned, hurt. 'Don't do that?'

'What?'

'Pull away.'

'Did I?'

For answer she closed her fingers about his arm and squeezed it, rubbing the inside of her thigh up and down his leg; closer now so that the tips of her breasts were grazing the hair on his chest.

'Tell me what you've been thinking of.'

Herne shook his head and looked over towards the window.

'I want to know.'

'It's none of your business!'

She moved her hand and leg away as if stung and turned quickly from him. Herne pushed back the covers and sat on the edge of the bed. The light through the shutters made slanting patterns over his legs.

He stood up and went to the window: opened one of the shutters and looked out. The side of the house, the place opposite; further up into town the outline of the top storey of The Cattlemen's House.

He stayed there for some time, listening to Josie shifting on the mattress behind him. After a while he got cold and went back and slipped under the covers.

Her warmth drew him like a magnet. He pushed against the roundness of her behind, let his head fall against the curve of her neck as she shifted her face round to kiss him. His cheek, his nose, his mouth. Hands reaching for him.

'God, Jed Herne, I swear you can keep as silent as you like. Just so long as you're here next to me. I feel so safe when I'm with you, Jed. So safe.'

He put the palm of his hand to her nipple and watched as her eyes closed. There was suddenly a double explosion as two shots ripped through the woodwork of the door. Herne's heart stopped for a fraction of a second, then he was pushing Josie across the bed and rolling backwards, one hand grasping upwards for the Colt at the bed head.

As he fell to the floor a third shot ploughed through the door and then another. From his knees, Herne replied twice and then made a leap at the door and kicked it back.

The lock shattered and sprang apart, the wood gave at the centre. The door rocked back on one hinge and Herne stepped out into the darkness of the small corridor.

His eyes struggled to become accustomed to the light; darker here than in the room. Herne thought he saw a shape at the end of the space and fired into it. Nothing moved or fell, and then from somewhere else there was a scurrying of movement and the sound of feet on boards.

Herne snapped off a shot and ran for the stairs. Two,

three paces and he was there. Below a door slammed. Herne took the steps in four jumps and opened the door, the handle awkward in his hand.

In the street nothing stirred. The moon showed the fronts of buildings, hitching posts, a deserted boardwalk. He became conscious of sounds behind him, people waking, lanterns being lit. He turned to go back into the house, a naked man with a Colt .45 in his hand.

Upstairs, Herne pulled on some clothes and knelt on the bed. People were standing outside and he shouted at them to get away and wait. He grasped Josie's shoulders and turned her over, feeling the resistance of her body. Her right arm fell sideways from her chest and onto his leg; its fingers were wet with what he knew was blood. One of the shots had gone into her below the rib cage and the soft flesh was sticking here and there to the sheet. Another shell had pierced her breast, drilled through it and pulled away a flap of skin that hung loosely about the wound.

Herne knelt up and gazed at what he could see of Josie in the light that still seeped into the room. He used the thumb of his right hand to shut her eye-lids. The thumb was stained with her blood and left a pattern on the skin, so that her closed eyes resembled crimson butterflies.

So safe, she had said. So safe.

'Mister Herne, I . . .'

He got off the bed. Grabbed his coat and a box of shells. Pushed his way through the people who had crowded round the door.

The old man was asleep in the livery stables and he didn't wake as Herne led his horse out into the night.

It was getting near dawn by the time Herne got close to the Broken Bar. The first strained signs of light were ringing the horizon and here and there were spurts of deepish red, heralds to the dawn. He rode well clear of the ranch buildings, taking a path round to the wind pump a hundred yards or more to the rear.

Herne tied up the horse and checked his Colt and the bayonet that he had sheathed inside his right boot. He was wearing a wool coat against the early morning chill which he buttoned tight as he started to walk slowly forwards.

There was a fence round the back of the house and a worn track that led to a door. The door was unlocked. Herne shut it behind him and stood inside, looking around, trying to get his bearings.

The room where he and Hastings had talked before was through towards the front of the house. He remembered a staircase and guessed that Hastings would sleep upstairs.

He wondered if the rancher slept alone.

There were three doors on the upper floor and the first of them led into a cupboard. The second was locked and Herne didn't want to break it down unless he had to.

His left hand closed round the handle to the third room and the other rested on the butt of the Colt. He eased the door open and went in, silent but fast. The room was long and large. There was a double bed with the covers pulled back as if whoever had been sleeping there had already risen for the day. The same crude and heavy furniture that Herne remembered from downstairs.

It was Clifford Hastings' room all right. Strange that a man so particular about his dress should choose to live in such sombre surroundings.

Herne's thoughts were interrupted by a noise from the ground floor. He went to the bedroom door and looked out. Seeing nothing, he closed the door behind him and went to the stairs. A light, which he had not noticed before, shone from underneath the door to the room where he and Hastings had last met.

Herne took his time getting there, stepping as carefully as he could. Yet soon the rest of the ranch would come to life and Herne would have too many guns to face, too much to do in too little time.

When he opened the door, Hastings seemed to be waiting for him. Waiting for someone. He was sitting in a chair just past the centre of the room and was fully dressed, except for his suit jacket.

His left hand was resting on the thigh of his left leg, fingers parted like a claw.

In the other hand he held a pistol that Herne recognised as a Smith and Wesson Schofield .45. A butt that was more curved than his own Colt, a thicker, more clumsy-looking barrel with a rounded section just ahead of the chamber. Not a gun that Herne would ever choose to use, an awkward single-action model, but one which Jesse James was said to have favoured.

Jesse James and Clifford Hastings both.

'I could shoot you down here and now as a robber and thief.'

'You could try.'

'I see very little to stop me.'

'Go ahead.'

Herne's hand was by his gun butt, fingers curled and ready; his body automatically dropped into a crouch. Hastings stared at him and the expression on the rancher's face told him that Hastings wasn't going to use his gun. Not then.

'I thought you only got others to do your killing for you.' Herne's voice was like a whip, cracking out at Hastings from the far side of the room.

'Meaning?'

'You know damn well! Part of it we talked about before—Tolly, Curly Young. That was your men. Same as the bunch that tried to take me right after we was talkin' here. And now there's the girl.'

For the first time, the expression on Hastings' face changed. He flinched visibly, letting the hand holding the gun drop an inch.

'What girl?'

'Name's Josie. Was Josie. Worked for Faulkner at The

Cattlemen's House.'

'Well, what about her? What's she got to do with me or the Broken Bar?'

The fingers of the left hand were opening and closing slowly, as if with a will of their own. Hastings blinked, not once, but several times.

'Tonight,' Herne said grimly, 'back in Liberation. Someone tried to gun me down in my bed. They shot the girl. Killed her.'

'I still don't see . . .'

Herne moved towards him and Hastings thought the big man was going to keep coming until he was upon him. His thin body pushed back into the chair and the gun hand shook a little.

'Soon as I left here yesterday some of your men tried to jump me an' it didn't succeed. So what happens next? Some feller tried a few shots through the bedroom door. It all points to you, Hastings.'

The white face shook from side to side in denial. The fingers of the left hand moved more and more frantically. Hastings' brown eyes flickered with something close to fear. Herne didn't think it was an emotion the Broken Bar man experienced very often.

'That in town with the girl. It was nothing to do with me. I swear it. I . . .'

'You're lyin'!'

'No, I'm . . .'

'I said you're lyin'!'

Hastings moved the Smith and Wesson and Herne lashed out at it with his free hand, sending it flying out of Hastings' grasp and across the room.

'No, don't . . .'

'That's right, mister. Don't!'

Herne had failed to hear the door open behind him or the man come in.

'Stand right still and let me see that gun of yorn on the floor. Now! Before this finger of mine gets carried away an' I pump a couple of shells into your back.'

Herne looked over his shoulder. Seth was leaning back against the door, his own Colt pointing at the middle of Herne's body. There was an expression of triumph on his face.

'You heard me. Let's see that gun on the ground. Easy now.'

Herne turned slowly towards Seth, using forefinger and thumb to lift the heavy pistol from its holster.

'That's right. Now let it go.'

Herne began to bend with it, as if placing it on the floor, his eyes never leaving Seth's face.

'That's it, you can drop . . .'

The Colt fell the short distance onto the worn carpet and Herne's body straightened up like a whiplash. But the hand that had dropped the gun didn't come back up empty. It had the hilt of the bayonet in it and midway through the movement the blade was unleashed across the room.

Seth's mouth stayed open, words drained in mid-sentence; he moved the gun to fire but something plunged its way through his shoulder blade and pinned him to the door. His hand opened in spite of itself and the pistol slipped out.

Hastings had dived for his own gun as soon as he saw what happened to his man. Herne, turning fast, had gone with him. The two landed almost side by side, struggling for possession of the Smith and Wesson.

Something kicked into Herne's groin and he let go of Hastings' arm for a moment. The gun was pulled away and then Herne struck out with his fist and the gun fell to the floor again as Hastings rolled back and into a chair. Herne jumped after him, clubbing him hard and sending the chair crashing over. Herne knelt above the rancher and grasped him by the front of his shirt. The eyes pleaded with him and as they did so Herne let him have two jabs to the side of the face. The head went lolling back and

Herne stood up, letting Hastings drop to the floor.

Only then did he notice the high-pitched sound coming from the door. Seth was trying to lever the bayonet out of his body, but he was getting weaker at every moment and every effort to move the blade merely made it cut deeper into his flesh and enlarged the wound.

'Take . . . ta . . . t . . .'

Herne went over to him. The blood that ran down his shirt front was joined by a steady drip, drip from behind. Seth's face was white with agony and fear and the effect of the rapid loss of blood.

'Take the . . .'

Herne set his left hand alongside the entry point of the bayonet and Seth screamed; he caught hold of the handle and the man screamed all the louder; he pulled the blade free with one tug and the scream cut off as though a gag had been placed across the man's mouth.

Seth put a hand out in front of him and Herne stepped to one side; the cowboy staggered forward; choked; began to fall; fainted into unconsciousness.

Herne stooped and picked up Seth's gun and tucked it into his belt; then he picked up his own Colt and holstered it. A moaning and a scuffling from the other end of the room told him that Hastings was coming round.

When he did come to, Herne was standing over him, waiting. 'What's it to be?'

Hastings wiped at his face, bringing his hand to the front to examine the few drops of blood that had fallen from his cut mouth. Herne repeated his question but the rancher still looked dazed.

Herne went out to the kitchen and returned with a jug of water that he threw in Hastings' face.

'What's it goin' to be, Hastings?'

'I don't . . . under . . . stand.'

Herne slapped him with the back of one hand, sending the rancher's head sideways and back.

'There's men gettin' killed all the time, Hastings. Killed

an' wounded. An' mostly on your say-so. When's it goin' t' stop?' He lifted the thin man half out of the chair and shook him like a dog with a rat.

'What . . . what do you want?'

'Start off with, you can write a statement sayin' that your men killed Tolly an' Curly Young on your orders.'

Hastings began to protest, but Herne lifted him up and pushed him towards the desk at the side of the room. 'You get to it, 'fore I fetch that bayonet to your stubborn hide.'

Hastings took a sheet of paper and a pen. He opened an ink well and began to write. Herne watched him for a while, then went over to where Seth was showing signs of life. He took out his Colt and reversed it, clubbing him back into unconsciousness. Hastings was still bent over the desk, scratching away frantically at the piece of paper.

'Hurry it along, will you!'

Very soon the rest of the ranch would be clamouring around outside and likely someone would spot Herne's horse.

Hastings coughed and bent lower; he opened a drawer and reached inside; his hand came out with a long envelope.

'I said move it along!'

Herne glanced at the window: it was almost light.

'Here it is.'

Herne turned at the sound of Hastings' voice; saw the little gun and leaped aside even as the report rang out. Something tugged at his shirt and a sharp pain cut his side as his right hand dived for the Colt and brought it up in a blur of speed. In the middle of that curve of movement there was a flash of flame and Clifford Hastings went backwards off his chair with a bullet in the centre of his chest.

In the short time it took Herne to cross to him, Hastings' eyes were already glazing over and when he tried to speak blood emerged in the place of words.

He lifted a hand with a great effort and beckoned Herne

closer. 'I never . . . the girl . . . had nothing to do . . .'

He broke into a racking cough which made his body arch forward and his head jolt back. Both arms came out, reaching for something that wasn't there. Long, thin fingers, still grasping in their last movement.

Clifford Hastings collapsed back, rolling over onto his side. Herne stood over him and watched the final twitching motions of death. Then he picked the rancher up and strode from the room towards the front of the house.

Men were running towards it, some still in their long johns, pulling on their gun belts. When they saw Herne standing with their employer's body in his arms they stopped and stared.

'I got a paper signed by Hastings sayin' the responsibility for Tolly an' Curly's deaths was his. An' now he's paid fer it. Seth's inside with a wound in him, but he'll patch up an' live.' He surveyed them as they stood their ground, watching him with obvious hostility. 'Seems to me any of you'd be a damn fool to throw his life away fer someone who's dead. Ain't even goin' t' pay no bills no more. Any of you think different?'

He looked at one face after another. They didn't like him none. Plumb hated him. But they knew he was talkin' sense.

'All right. He's your boss. You bury him.'

And he dropped Hastings' dead body on the dirt in front of them. Then he backed away until he was at the side of the house before turning and walking to where he'd left his horse.

Every now and then he glanced round, but none of them saw fit to follow.

By the time Herne had arrived back in Liberation everyone was going about his or her normal daily business. He rode down to the livery stable, then walked back to the marshal's office.

The boy from the stable was there, sitting in Dan Stewart's chair. When Herne walked in on him, he leapt up like his rear end had found a cactus and blushed redder than sunset.

'What you doin' here, boy?'

'Please, Mister Herne, I'm sorry but, I'm sorry but . . .'

'Spit it out, son, before it chokes you.'

'Marshal Stewart, he asked me to stay here and give you a message.'

'Well, what is it?'

'He's gone out to the Double C ranch. Miss Emerson, she sent in a rider askin' for him. Real early. He says you're to wait here till he comes back. Lessn' he don't come back by a hour after noon.'

Herne made a face to show his annoyance. 'What'm I supposed to do then?'

The boy gulped and shook his head, eyes wide. 'I don't know, Mister Herne, marshal he didn't say.'

'Okay, son, get out of here. My horse is down to the stable. You curry him well. Understand?'

'Yes, Mister Herne. Yes, sir.'

Herne took a coin from his pocket and the boy caught it as it tossed through the air.

'Now, on your way.'

As the office door was shut, Herne took off his coat and hung it on one of the pegs on the wall. He stretched, realised he was hungry, and thought that in a minute or two he'd walk over to The Cattlemen's House for a bite to eat.

It took a whole three seconds before he remembered that Josie wouldn't be there to cook it.

CHAPTER ELEVEN

Bathsheba Emerson stood at the upstairs window and watched the trail of dust grow larger, closer and closer. So he had heeded her message; he had decided to come. And alone.

He rode tall in the saddle, riding like a man with a purpose but without any unnecessary haste. Bathsheba watched him as he passed the corral and the outbuildings, her green eyes following him all the way to the hitching pole outside the ranch house.

As he got down from his horse, she noted for maybe the hundredth time the set of his shoulders, the slim strength of his hips. The brown moustache curved round his mouth drawing attention to lips that Bathsheba had known only in her dreams of him.

She watched him step towards the door, one hand pressed against her thigh, the other fidgeting with a gold pendant she wore over her yellow blouse, the back of her wrist pushing against the lower curve of her breast.

After several moments she turned and walked to the stairs: he was standing below in the hallway, looking up as if knowing she were about to make her appearance.

'Marshal. It was so good of you to come.'

Dan Stewart nodded briefly and stood back as Bathsheba came down the stairs. Besides the yellow blouse, she was wearing a black skirt that fitted snugly at the hips and thighs, then flared out round the calves. Shiny black boots showed beneath the hem. Her long, dark hair glistened as she moved.

'Let's go in here, marshal.'

She opened the door to the best room and stood aside for him to enter first. As he walked past her she moved slightly so that his arm brushed against the front of her body. Bathsheba's eyes closed for an instant and a sigh echoed inside her head.

'In a little while, we'll have coffee, marshal. I'll make it for you myself.'

Stewart shifted around uneasily in his chair. 'I don't have the time, Miss Emerson, there's a lot to do back in town.'

She raised an eyebrow quizzically. 'Don't you have a deputy?'

'Sure, but . . .'

'Well, then, I'm positive he can handle things for you.' She smiled slowly. 'It's a long while since we talked, marshal, just the two of us.' The smile broadened and he could see the tip of her tongue between her red lips. 'Or may I call you Dan now?'

Stewart stood up suddenly and gazed around the room.

'Don't worry, marshal, most of the men are out on the range.' Bathsheba got up from her chair and began to walk across the carpet towards him. 'Don't worry, Dan.'

He stepped past her and stood with his back to the window, the sunlight warming him through his black waistcoat and white shirt. 'You wanted to see me urgent.'

'Very well. If we must get straight to business: I've been thinking over what you said yesterday about leaving Hastings and the Broken Bar to the law.'

'And?'

'And I've decided that you're right.'

'That's good, Miss Emerson.'

'Bathsheba.'

'Sorry, I . . .'

'Call me Bathsheba, Dan. While we're alone—and friends. We are friends, aren't we?'

She was moving towards him again, closing on him slowly, like a hunter towards its prey, body tense and eyes alive.

'Bathsheba, then. I'm right pleased you've decided to leave things to me. That's the way it's got to be.'

'But there is a little proposition I'd like to make to you, Dan.'

She was standing directly in front of him and he could smell the sweetness of her breath and the slightly cloying scent of her perfume. The skin of her neck seemed to shine.

'Go ahead.'

'You're only one man, strong as you might be. And you've only one deputy. That's never enough against Hastings. You deputise my men. Say, a dozen of them. Then you can ride in and finish off the Broken Bar for ever.'

'That's all you're interested in, isn't it? Getting rid of the Broken Bar. You ain't worried about law an' order. You ain't even worried about me, whatever you pretend. You just want to see Hastings an' his ranch wiped off the map of this territory. That's it, ain't it?'

Dan Stewart's face was red with anger; the birthmark on his cheek showed clearly. Bathsheba's eyes sparkled, then dimmed. She put out a hand and touched Stewart's arm lightly with one finger.

'It isn't true, Dan. Especially that I don't care about you.'

He threw up his arm and knocked her hand away. 'Damn it, woman, can't you never do nothin' but lie? Why the hell d'you think all you have to do is make up to me an' everythin'll be just like you want it? You reckon that's all you got to do, don't you? Make an offer of that body of yorn an' men'll go out an' get theirselves killed for you!'

She stepped away, eyes blazing now, face flushed; her hands tight in clenched fists, nails digging into her palms.

'How dare you talk to me like that? How dare you suggest that I would . . .'

Stewart came towards her: 'Bathsheba, you'd do any damned thing you could to get rid of Hastings and what I'd like to know is why? What did he do to you that you can't forgive?' He stared at her with scorn. 'What wouldn't he do?'

She sprang at him, with her open hand clawing for his face but Stewart ducked his head back and grabbed her wrist and held it firmly.

'He spurned you, didn't he, Bathsheba. He turned you down and that's one thing you can't stand. So you'll get round me as a way of gettin' your own back. An' you'll try to get your men deputised so that they can go in and shoot down the Broken Bar, all legal like.'

Both of them were breathing heavily, perspiring freely. Dan felt her arm tense in his grip, then relax.

'You can let me go now,' she said quietly.

He did so and they continued to stand there, avoiding looking directly at each other. Then Bathsheba turned away and went to the door; she walked out of the room, leaving him there alone.

Dan Stewart paced the carpet, knowing that he could leave, should leave, yet not going. Something kept him there still, a sense of things unfinished, maybe unsaid. After a short time she returned with a coffee tray.

Her face looked fresh and undisturbed, her eyes moved over his as if nothing had happened between them, no anger, no pent-up violence.

She set down the tray and asked him to come over and sit down; poured out his coffee and passed it to him with a smile.

'Is that sweet enough for you?' she said a minute or so later.

'Sure,' Stewart nodded, 'it's fine.'

He thought she was about to get out of her chair and go over to him, but she didn't. All she did was set her cup down in its saucer and stare over at him, the expression on her face both serious and innocent. It made her seem a lot younger than her forty-odd years: Stewart wondered how often she practiced it in front of her mirror.

'What you said about Clifford, Dan, about Clifford Hastings. I guess you've heard all the rumours. It's true we were betrothed to be married at one time. Two weeks before the ceremony—church and fancy party all arranged—it was called off.'

Now she did come to him and knelt beside his chair, looking up into his eyes. A tress of warm, dark hair fell against his arm, but he didn't move.

'One thing you must believe, Dan. It wasn't Clifford who called it off. It was me. I did it myself, Dan, and do you know why? I realised I couldn't marry him because... because I knew that I didn't love him.' She lowered her head and for an instant Stewart thought she was going to cry, but when he saw her eyes again they were clear as before. 'It would have given us one of the biggest ranches in this part of the country, maybe the biggest. All that wealth, all that power and I turned my back on it, Dan. Out of a lack of one little thing... a lack of love.'

Bathsheba let her face move nearer to him, a hand rested lightly, warmly on his arm and he could feel the shape of her fingers clearly through the thin material of his white shirt.

'You can understand that, can't you, Dan? You can understand about loving?'

'Sure,' he answered slowly, 'I can understand, but...'

She placed a finger against his mouth: 'No, Dan, no buts. Not now. Not for us. You must see, you and I, Dan, together we can have what we want. We can have each other and...'

Stewart brushed her finger away. 'We can have nothing, Bathsheba. Nothing!'

'Dan!'

'You talked about love, how things won't work without

it. That's enough.'

'But I love you, Dan, You must see that. Know it. Feel it deep within you. It's deep within me, Dan, I . . .'

Stewart sprang up from the chair and headed for the door, his face taut and white. Bathsheba ran after him, grabbing at his arm, attempting to stop him, to pull him back.

'Let go!'

'Dan! Listen to me!'

'I have listened. Listened till I'm sick of the sound of your voice, your smell, the sight of you.'

'No!'

She wailed her cry and flung herself in front of him, both arms tight about his neck, legs pressed hard against his body. He struggled with her but she held fast as if she was holding onto the most precious thing in her life, onto life itself.

'For Christ's sake, let me go!'

He yanked one of her arms away and she held him all the tighter with the other, lifting her face towards his, her eyes, her mouth filling his vision. Then her lips were pressed onto his and he felt her tongue forcing its way into his mouth like a lizard, a snake.

He tried to shout at her and as his lips parted she was kissing him long and deep.

'Jesus!'

He grabbed at her hair and pulled her face away from his own, stared at her, then wiped at his mouth with his free hand and spat down onto the carpet.

'That's what I think of you, Bathsheba. You and every other blasted woman I ever met.'

'That's right!' she sneered. 'That's right. You ain't a real man at all. No real man would wipe off a woman's kisses that way. You ain't natural, Dan Stewart, you just ain't natural!'

He slapped her face, twice, making her head rock back and forth with ringing blows that brought fresh blood from the side of her mouth.

She banged her bunched fist at his arm and as he went to fend her off, she pulled the Remington .44 free from the holster at his chest.

Stewart stared down at the barrel, inches away from him, her two hands on the butt now, holding it as steady as her nerves and excitement would allow.

'Now kiss me, Dan Stewart, now kiss me before I blow a hole in you for being the bastard you are!'

He saw her fingers begin to tighten on the trigger and bowed his head towards her own, closing his eyes as her mouth moved over his. He felt the warmth of her lips and smelt her perfume more powerfully than before; her tongue was probing inside him again and this time he could taste her blood from where he had hit her. Salt richness of her blood.

Stewart moved his hands quickly, reaching for her arms, for the gun. She grabbed at his waistcoat with one hand, biting down on his lower lip, clinging to him.

There was an explosion that seemed to fill the room and both bodies rocked apart, then collapsed against each other. For several seconds they performed a strange, slow dance, feet unmoving, bodies swaying in time to some silent rhythm.

Then Bathsheba began to slide towards the floor, the gun still in her hand. Stewart stepped away from her, staring at her face as it looked up at him in wonder. He moved his head and gazed down at his chest.

The front of his waistcoat was singed with the firing of the gun and a dark circle of blood centred round his breastbone. He lifted up his hand and saw that it, too, was thick with blood.

Bathsheba Emerson was on her knees, trying to keep her head inclined upwards so that she could see Stewart. But it was a struggle she was losing with every second; with every second that her life poured from the gaping wound at the top of her blouse, between the V of the gold pendant.

What had been the shiny skin of her neck . . .

What had been living flesh . . .

The gun tumbled at last from her grasp and hit the carpet with a dull thud. Stewart gazed down at her and her eyes sought him out for a last time.

Found him: flickered: faded: died.

How long Dan Stewart stood there he wasn't certain. It seemed like far longer than it could have really been. At last he picked up his gun from the floor and replaced it in his holster. There was someone shouting from outside the front door. Stewart walked through and opened it, still slightly dazed.

A man in his sixties stood there with a hammer in one hand and a old rifle in the other.

'Hitch up a wagon!'

'I don't know, marshal. I . . .'

'Hitch up a damned wagon!'

And Stewart turned on his heel and went back into the house. It was going to be a long ride back into town. Long and lonely—with only a dead woman for company.

It was a strange sight: the marshal sitting up in front of the wagon, bolt upright, looking straight ahead and paying no attention to those folk who clamoured towards him from both sides.

His face was set, blank, pale with strain.

Behind him, lying in the bottom of the wagon, was the mistress of the Double C ranch. Bathsheba Emerson, her long dark hair combed out on either side of her face; eyes closed, refusing the sun.

A white sheet had been used to cover her body, lain over her with the hem touching her neck.

As the people of Liberation realised the grisly contents of Stewart's wagon, they stepped back for a moment, stunned and silent. Then curiosity grew and they pushed forward again, anxious for a glimpse of the dead woman's body, eager to ask the Marshal for information.

Herne was down at the far end of the street when Stewart arrived. He walked steadily up towards the office, seeing the crowd gather and uncertain in his mind what the reason might be.

Then he saw Dan Stewart and the wagon and thought he knew.

Hoped that he was wrong, but inwardly knew that he was right. Two ranch owners, two of the most powerful people in the territory, and both dead in so short a space of time.

Without them, the trouble could just blow over—but Herne didn't feel it that way.

He stepped up onto the boardwalk and almost knocked over a small boy who was scuttling through the outside of the mob to get a better view.

'Hey, sonny!' Herne caught hold of him by the shoulder. 'Why don't you watch where you're goin'?'

The boy struggled, then realised who had hold of him. His eyes popped and he stared up at Herne in a mixture of fear and wonder. 'Gosh, marshal, I didn't mean nothin'. I just wanted to see who Marshal Stewart had killed now. My pa, he says that you an' Marshal Stewart are goin' to kill half the town before you're done.'

His blue eyes flickered over Herne's face. 'Is that right, marshal? Are you and Marshal Stewart really goin' to kill half the town?'

Herne's fingers gripped the boy's shoulder until he cried out with surprise and pain. Then he let him go and stood and watched him as he scrabbled his way through the crowd of adults that had thickened even further.

Damn! said Herne to himself. Sweet damn!

And he made a path for himself to the wagon.

Stewart was instructing a group of the townsfolk to lift Bathsheba from the back of the wagon and take her over the street to the undertaker's. His face was still taut and pale; Herne thought it was he first time he had seen any sign of real worry and caught a sudden glimpse of how Stewart would look if he lived to get old.

Old as he was himself.

Old as his pa, Long John Stewart, stone blind in Omaha: waiting for the coming of the rainbow whose colours he'd never be able to see again.

'Come on, folks, it's over now. There ain't nothin' left t' see. Get on about your business.'

Herne stood sternly by the head of the wagon, staring down into the crowd, waiting while it broke up into little groups of twos or threes.

At the back of the throng he saw the portly figure of Wilbur Merz and beyond him, standing in the doorway of The Cattlemen's House, Quentin Faulkner.

He wondered just how the town council would greet this latest death. Whether they would be relieved or angry. He guessed that before very long he and Stewart would get to know.

He glanced round at Dan, still standing by the door to the office, his eyes unusually dull and revealing nothing. At that moment maybe seeing as little as his old man.

Herne turned and went over to him, put his hand to Stewart's arm: 'Come on, Dan, let's get inside.'

They sat and drank coffee laced with whisky for the best part of an hour, saying little all the while. After that hour had gone there was a knocking on the door and Herne opened it to let in the banker, Merz, and some of the town council. Faulkner was not amongst them.

They stood round looking important and disapproving while Stewart recounted the basic events that had taken place at the Emerson ranch. When he had finished, they waited, expecting more by way of explanation. Realising there was to be none, Wilbur Merz patted his belly and took a step forward. Like he was about to address a meeting.

'I think you should, er, understand our position, marshal. We hired you to keep the peace in this territory. Now being responsible with your deputy here for the deaths of two such important folk as Clifford Hastings and Bathsheba Emerson rings strangely when seen in terms of maintaining the peace. The Double C and the Broken Bar are responsible for a goodly share of the prosperity of Liberation ...'

'An' a hell of a lot of its trouble,' put in Herne, but the banker ignored him, addressing his remarks to Stewart.

'It is only fair to tell you that the council will have to call an official meeting of all its members to reconsider your appointment.'

Merz hurrumphed and hemmed and hawed and made a whole lot more strange sounds, but still Stewart made no obvious reaction. Finally, Merz stood back and looked at the other men in his party. All were decidedly uncomfortable. Herne got up and pushed open the door.

'Okay, you said your piece. Now get your asses out of here.'

'Really, that is no way to ...'

Herne's hand moved towards his gun. 'I told you to get!'

Merz nodded quickly and waddled through the door, the rest following close behind. Herne slammed the door so hard and fast that the last member of the council was almost knocked off his feet.

He poured two more shots of whisky into their mugs and swilled water round the coffee grounds. Much as he would have liked to avoid it, there were questions he himself wanted to ask of Dan Stewart.

'Dan, I guess you don't want to talk about this business, but ...'

Stewart looked over at him with tired eyes: 'Go ahead, Jed. I owe you answers. More than them parasites.' He stared at the door in disgust.

'This thing with the Emerson woman, how she got shot.

You said she grabbed for your gun and in the struggle it went off—what was goin' on before that, Dan? What was it she wanted to see you about so all-fired sudden?'

'She wanted me to deputise her men. Go in and shoot Hastings out. She didn't know what you just now told me about him bein' dead.'

Herne nodded, stood with one foot on the seat of the chair, not wanting to sit down. 'That's all, Dan? Nothin' personal?'

Stewart blinked, then looked at the floor. After a while he said quietly: 'What difference does it make, Jed?'

'Damn! It sure makes a difference to me. If'n you fought with her 'cause she was tryin' to put a bullet through you that's one thing. If'n it was over somethin' between you an' her, that might be somethin' else.'

Stewart stood up fast, knocking his chair back. 'Say what you mean, Jed. Stop stallin'.'

'All right. There's bin a lot of rumours flyin' round. Remarks folk've made. Things you've said yourself about women that just don't seem right. Don't seem ...'

The words slid off his tongue into silence.

Stewart came closer to him, blood back in his cheeks. 'Normal, Jed, that the word you're lookin' for. Don't seem normal. Say it, Jed. Say it!'

Herne stood to his full height. 'I asked you before what happened back in Ogden to make you quit. You wouldn't say. If'n it was over some shootin' I reckon you'd have come out with it. First, I thought it was somethin' over a woman. But, no, it weren't that. Not a woman, Dan. Trouble all right. But over a man.'

The atmosphere inside the room was like the silent, still moment before the storm breaks. The two men stood facing one another, hands never far from their guns, eyes locked across the short distance between them.

Finally, Stewart relaxed and looked away. 'Yes, that's right. A man. Young feller who worked behind the bar in the saloon. Folk got to know how I ... how I felt about him. Took my badge an' run me out of town.'

The last few words were almost too soft to be heard. Herne stood there, looking at the man he had thought of as his friend, finding it impossible to stop the waves of disgust that were running through him.

Stewart walked over to the jail door then turned around. 'I'm glad I said it, Jed. Not many folks I could have come out with it to. Not like that. But I'm glad I did.' He spread his hands wide for a moment, then let them fall back by his sides. 'If'n you want to quit, that's okay by me. I'll understand. My job here's on the line anyhow. An' with Hastings and the Emerson woman gone, I don't reckon there'll be too much trouble. No more than I can handle.'

Herne stood there, looking at him and listening, scarcely taking it in.

Stewart came towards him: 'Thanks for your help, Jed. Maybe we'll run into one another again some time.'

He held out his hand: Herne looked down at it for a second, then spun round on his heel and walked out, leaving Stewart standing there, fingers outstretched, seeking friendship.

CHAPTER TWELVE

The owner of The Five Aces wasn't any too pleased to have Jed Herne patronising his place. Herne knew it and he didn't care: he didn't give a damn.

The Cattlemen's House was too big; there would be too many folk hanging around, all wanting to ask fool questions. Herne wasn't interested in answering others' questions. Right now he had enough of his own.

He'd taken the bottle and glass from the surly saloon owner without a word; dropped coins onto the wet, stained counter and pushed chairs out of the way till he reached a table over by the wall. He sat down and rocked the seat back so that it was perched on its back legs, his shoulders resting against the wooden boards.

He saw the few regular drinkers looking at him while pretending not to. Sensing his mood and not daring to do anything that might cross him. Herne let them do what they wanted. Just sat and drank. Not heavily, not quickly. A steady, absorbed drinking while daylight ran through and began to change into night.

What else was happening while he was sitting there Herne didn't care. What Dan Stewart was doing or thinking he didn't care either. Why the hell should he?

Herne felt betrayed. He had known Stewart as a friend, an open, honest man worthy of riding alongside, fighting with—maybe even dying with if it came to it.

And now something stuck in the back of his throat that tasted bitter as gall.

Damn him!

Herne slammed his fist down onto the table and sent his glass flying, whisky spilling across the surface of the wood and onto the floor.

Men turned and stared and Herne ignored them; he got up and scooped up the glass; refilled it; drank.

Oil lamps had been lit and the smoke from them drifted up to the ceiling, the smell mingling with that of spilt beer and stale tobacco smoke. No girls in pretty green dresses here, no roulette wheels or faro tables. Only a solitary whore in torn, shabby clothes and a pack of cards at the end of the bar for anyone who fancied a game to take and use.

Men mostly came to The Five Aces to drink, not to gamble or socialise.

Herne stretched. Glancing down, he saw the deputy marshal's badge still pinned to his chest. He pulled it off, tearing the front of his shirt, and tossed it into the middle of the room. The badge clinked, rolled, came to a halt in a puddle of slops and spit.

'That ain't goin' to save you!'

The voice was high, young. Herne let his chair come forward onto four legs, hand moving away from the bottle towards his hip. Yes, he could see him now. Hadn't noticed him come in. Standing by the end of the bar closest to the door.

The kid from the Double C.

The one who he'd talked down that night in The Cattlemen's House; from whom he had taken the pair of guns.

Well, now he'd got fresh ones. There in the twin holsters, worn too low just like before.

The kid looked over at Herne, his gaze made disturbing by the cast in the right eye. Spiky hair jutting up from his head, the weak moustache shaved clean.

'Throwin' that badge ain't goin' t' help.'

Herne looked at him and knew that shooting it out with

him was the last thing he wanted. Now. Now he didn't trust himself too well, his reactions or his reasons.

'You got too much to pay for. An' I'm goin' t' see you do.'

'Kid, I come in here fer a drink. You do the same or get on out. I ain't got no quarrel with you, not any more.'

The youngster's fingers almost touched his right hand gun, then pulled clear as though aware he was making his move too soon.

'I told you, you ain't talkin' your way out of it. Not again. You did that to me before but not this time. I ain't goin' t' let no man talk me out of a fight again. You understand that?'

His left hand was pointing directly at Herne, the right grazing his gun butt.

Herne sighed and lifted the glass to his lips and sank the last of the whisky. 'I hear you, kid. Bleatin' like somethin' that ain't bin weaned.'

'Don't you talk t'me like that, you bastard!'

Herne pushed the table to one side and stood up. Everyone in the murky saloon was watching him. Herne's eyes flickered over them all, checking them out to see if the kid had any support. For a couple of seconds his eyes rested on the owner at his place behind the bar.

There was one man who'd be plumb happy to see Herne get his. Jed wondered if he wanted that enough to take a hand himself. Asked himself if the shotgun from beneath the counter had been replaced.

'C'mon! Let's get to it!'

The kid took a couple of steps forward and most other folk automatically stepped back. Herne stood his ground. 'Son, I took your guns once an' I can do it again. Far as I'm concerned you an' me ain't got no fight. I'm through bein' marshal here an' soon as I done drinkin' this bottle here, I'm reckoning to be moving on. Let's leave it that way, 'cause . . .'

'Mister, I'm warnin' you, you ain't goin' t' talk your

way through me again.'

'... 'Cause if you carry on shooting yourself off at the mouth I'm goin' t' get so tired of the sound I drop you right there just to shut you up!'

The kid's right hand was resting on the wood of the butt and his left was almost as close. The expression on his face told Herne what was going to happen.

'Mister, I'm goin' t' fill you full of holes like I did that poxed-up woman of yorn. Lyin' in your bed like ...'

He never finished the sentence. Herne's hand dived for his Colt. The kid saw it and pulled at his guns. The right one was almost clear of the holster when the first shell struck him in the centre of that arm and shattered the bone. He stumbled back with a scream on his lips and tried to pull his other gun. Herne shifted his Colt and fired a second time. The bullet drilled through the kid's forearm and he howled with pain and let the pistol fall back into its holster.

'I was fer lettin' you live, son, but you opened that fool mouth of yorn once too often. You never should have told me what you did to that woman.'

He thumbed back the hammer of the gun.

Sensed a movement along the bar.

'Since when you bin particular about women gettin' killed, Mister? Why, that friend of yours, he shot himself one just this mornin'.'

The saloon owner moved his hands from under the edge of the bar and, right enough, the shotgun was there. The twin barrels swung round towards Herne and he watched them, judging his moment. As they came close to being level, Herne squeezed back on the trigger and the head above the shotgun disappeared in a blur of blood and bone.

Herne started to walk forward and as he did, he saw the kid moving from the corner of his eye.

'Don't try it!'

'I ain't goin' t' ...'

He held the pistol with both hands, the pain caused by doing so etched clearly on his face.

'You surely ain't!'

Herne fired twice and the kid was slammed back against the far wall. His eyes opened, the gun tilted forward on his finger end and then rolled off and bounced on the boards. The kid's head dropped down and he slid after his gun, shot twice close to the heart.

Herne reached for the spare shells at his gun belt and realised that Stewart was standing by the bat-wing doors. The two men looked at one another without emotion.

'You sure do have a way of sneakin' up on folk,' said Herne.

'You sure have a way of killin' people with that Colt.'

'If I have to.'

Stewart stepped into the saloon, looked at the kid slumped in the corner and at the other body draped over the bar. He saw Herne's badge lying on the floor.

'This weren't law business, then?'

'No. My business.'

'You reckon that might make it mine?'

'No. One of these two didn't give me a chance. The other wanted killin' anyway. Don't see that need bother you at all.'

He slid the Colt back into his holster and looked Stewart full in the face. Then he walked right by him and out into the street. His horse was waiting in the livery stable and he was going to get him and leave Liberation as fast as he could.

Dan Stewart didn't reckon that either the Broken Bar or the Double C would come rushing into town right off and call him out for a showdown. Why should they? The kind of fierce loyalty that they displayed towards one another was largely fuelled by the individuals who ran them. And with those two dead, most of the men wouldn't be too interested in getting shot at for lack of good reason.

Stewart guessed that mostly they'd stick around, getting ready for the big push of the trail herds down to Cheyenne. Just cowboys doing a job and waiting for the banks or someone to sell the property out. Then they'd see who the new owners were, decide to stay or leave, get fired or hired.

Of course, there might be the Double C ramrod to deal with. Stewart had an notion he was a man who'd himself taken more than just a shine to Bathsheba Emerson. So he didn't take any chances. He locked himself in back of the marshal's office that night, using the bunk bed behind the jail. Both his Colt and Remington were loaded and close to hand and the 10 gauge shotgun that he favoured was propped against the wall.

Stewart put off turning in as late as possible, thinking he would have difficulty getting to sleep, but it wasn't so. Almost as soon as his head touched the straw mattress, he was fast off.

Solid, impenetrable sleep: no dreams.

The first sounds, then, were real. Voices loud enough to cut through two walls, two sets of doors; stones falling against wood and brick and then the sound of smashing glass.

Stewart rolled off the bunk and reached for his pants, pulling them on fast. He pushed his arms into his shirt and wiped the sleep from the corners of his eyes.

Shotgun in hand, he unlocked the door from the jail to his front office. He could hear the men louder now but not yet what they were saying. Glass was scattered over the floor, where both of the windows had been smashed. Bars across them made it impossible for anyone to climb through. The outside door was still locked.

Stewart moved to the right-hand window and looked out. There were six, no, seven, men out there. Standing in the street. Armed with pistols at their belts and some with rifles in their hands. As he watched, Stewart saw one of them hurl a piece of rock towards the other window and flinched as the last of the glass splintered away.

'Come out, marshal. Out here where we can see you.'

One of the men brought his rifle to his shoulder and sent a bullet through the window close by where Stewart stood. It whined past him and buried itself in the wall opposite.

Stewart had underestimated the strength of feeling at the Double C. It wasn't just Miller, the ramrod, but half a dozen of the others as well.

'We know you're in there, marshal.'

Stewart set down the shotgun and drew the Colt from his side. He took quick aim and sent a shot into the dirt of the street only a few feet in front of Miller. Smiled when he saw the startled man jump back. Flattened himself against the wall in preparation for the answering barrage of fire.

'Show yourself, marshal, get outside!'

'Yeah, let's get a good shot at you!'

'All you're good for is killin' women, is that it? You afraid to fight like a man?'

He sent his second shot much closer, this time aiming at the next cowboy along from Miller. The third went in the other direction. At that the Double C boys scattered for cover.

But after a few moments, the shouts, the taunts began again.

Stewart could see that at the end of the street, beyond the last Double C man, the citizens of Liberation were arriving to watch their favourite sport.

He pushed shells into the chambers of his .45 and got ready to holler. 'What you want, Miller?'

'What d'you think?'

'That's what I'm askin'.'

'You, marshal. We want you—dead.'

'What for?'

'For Bath ... for Miss Emerson. You cowardly bastard!'

Stewart moved his pistol, trying to get a bead on the man, but he couldn't. Miller seemed to have slipped back out of sight behind the wall of The Cattlemen's House.

'You an' me, Miller. That what you want?'

'That's damned right!'

'What about your boys?'

'They'll hold off while you make your play.'

'An' after?'

Stewart heard Miller laugh. 'That won't worry you, marshal. On account of you bein' dead.'

'But if I ain't?'

'Then that's your problem. It sure won't be mine.'

Stewart weighed it up—not that it took long. If he chose to stay where he was there was plenty of ammunition, but there were enough of them and sufficient cover to wear him down. He couldn't hope to pick them all off. And sooner or later they'd get to him.

So ...

Stewart checked his guns one more time and yelled out loud and clear. 'All right, Miller, you got it your way. You and me, a straight shoot-out, face to face. Any one of your boys tried his hand an' he's likely to get dead afore I do. That understood?'

There was a pause and then Miller's voice: 'You got it, marshal. Now quit blabbin' an' get out here.'

Stewart stood back from the window and went to unbolt the door. He knew that the moment he stepped outside seven guns could open fire on him and cut him down without so much as a chance. But he set his faith in the strength of Scott Miller's desire for personal revenge. He alone would want to kill the man he thought responsible for his mistress' death.

To prove his worth as a man to her in death even though he couldn't when she was alive.

Stewart pushed open the door, paused: nothing happened. Down the street dogs were barking, but the townsfolk had fallen silent. He stepped onto the boardwalk and looked around.

Two of the Double C boys were fifty yards to the left, standing by the doorway of the saddler's. Another pair were closer on his right, standing well back on the same side of the main street as his own office. That left two unaccounted for—and Miller himself.

Stewart took a pace towards the street, staring over at the Cattlemen's House. 'All right, Miller, who's skulking round corners now?'

There was a word that Stewart couldn't properly hear and a movement close to the doors that led into the saloon. A handful of folk scurried off in either direction and Miller was standing there alone, returning Stewart's stare.

For several moments the two men faced one another without word or movement, then Miller slapped his riding whip hard against his leg. 'You killed her, marshal. Cut her down in cold blood and used that shield of yorn to hide behind. You ain't hidin' from me. Not this time.'

Stewart took a half-step forward and reached the edge of the boardwalk. He thought he picked out another of the Double C men in the crowd down to the left but he couldn't be sure.

'Stop your talkin',' he called across, 'an' make your play.'

Scott Miller stepped down from outside The Cattlemen's House and into the street. Began walking to his left, Stewart's right, taking slow, deliberate steps, watching the marshal closely all the time. Waiting for the first move.

Stewart too came down into the street and began to walk to his left, knowing that he had to keep the same distance between Miller and himself. Worried that it gave his back to the Double C cowboys at his rear.

He hoped he had judged the ramrod's motives right and

that the man's word would hold.

The barking grew louder until there was the sound of a stone striking home followed by a yelp and then silence. Just two men circling each other in the stillness of the early spring morning.

Miller watched the marshal's eyes, uncertain of which gun he would make a move for first. As for Stewart, he kept looking at Miller's left arm, knowing there was only one move he could make. Telling himself all the time that he was fast enough, that he could outdraw Miller, outshoot him.

Miller stopped.

He had curved two-thirds of the way across the street. Looking at him now, Stewart could see most of the front of the building that housed his office and the jail. The Cattlemen's House was only something at the corner of an eye.

It would be now, he told himself. He dropped his body deeper into a crouch; Miller did likewise. Inside both their heads a clock ticked time away and for one of them it would stop any . . .

Miller's left hand dived for his gun and Stewart slanted himself to the left and went for the Colt at his hip. The two guns seemed to come up together. A double flash, a joint roar and the crowd gasped and held its breath. Looked from one man to the other. Waited.

The Double C ramrod faltered back a step, then another. His vast, bull-like frame shook and he moved his head twice, quickly, then stared down back at Stewart.

The marshal had not moved. His Colt was steady in his right hand. Wherever Miller's bullet had gone, it had not hit him.

Miller started to sway on his feet, the large body threatening to collapse at any moment. It was possible to see the wound now, high to the side of the dark plaid shirt that he was wearing.

'You bastard! You miserable no-account bastard! I ain't goin' to be killed by you. I just ain't!'

He steadied himself and with a supreme effort raised his left arm.

'You ...'

Stewart had never altered his position. He shot the big man once in the chest and once in the head. Miller opened his mouth one more time, but all that came out was a dying breath and a choked cough of phlegm and clotted blood.

When he hit the dirt of the street the dust rose up in a thick cloud. A woman screamed and men shouted and something burnt into Stewart's right shoulder blade like a red-hot poker. He felt himself hurled forwards and as he went his left hand grabbed for the Remington at his chest.

Turning as he fell he caught a glimpse of Quentin Faulkner hurrying back from the second storey balcony of The Cattlemen's House.

Then he was on the ground and his back and shoulder were hurting like all hell and someone was firing at him but it wasn't Faulkner any more, it was one of the Double C. Earth spurted up and into his face and he flattened himself and tried to see who it was but all there was were running legs and a blur of colour and dirt choking his mouth and filling his eyes.

Stewart started to push himself towards the boardwalk but a jet of pain cut through the top half of his body and he closed his eyes fast. When he opened them again they were stinging with the dust that had been trapped inside them and there was someone coming up the street towards him, firing wildly with a rifle.

Stewart pushed up his body onto one knee and fired twice with the Remington, both times too fast. The shots pulled to one side and he could see the Double C cowboy was standing there now, taking more careful aim.

From another direction a shell burst the edge of the boardwalk immediately past him.

He tried to use his pistol but he couldn't seem to find

the strength to pull the trigger.

As he watched, the rifle that was aiming for him went suddenly up into the air and the man threw up one arm and fell onto his face as though he'd been kicked in the small of the back.

Through a maze of dust Stewart saw a man riding hell for leather towards him, hand slotting Sharps rifle back into place, steering the stallion over to his side of the street. Slowing. Bending in the saddle. Reaching out an arm. A hand.

Stewart reached up and caught hold fast and felt himself lifted up and onto the horse. The effort made him all but cry out and the pain wrenched through him, but he hauled himself round until he was behind the saddle and the big horse was galloping away to the far end of the street.

Shots traced after them and the rider slowed down again and turned into an alley close by the edge of town.

'Damn, Jed, I don't know ...' The sentence ended in a fit of coughing.

Herne reached round and helped Stewart to the ground. 'You save your breath. Think yourself lucky you still got the wherewithall to use it.'

Herne dismounted and pulled the Sharps to him; knelt by the end of the alley. After a few moments, one of the Double C men stuck out his head to see where Herne and the marshal had got to.

Herne put a bullet through his ear and made him duck back, clutching at the side of his head in agony and disbelief.

There were three at the far side, beyond The Cattlemen's House, ducked back alongside of a general store. He guessed there must be one on the same side that he and Stewart were waiting.

'How many should there be left?' he asked.

'Got one each so far. Leaves five.'

Herne nodded. 'Two on this side, then.'

'What d'you reckon, Jed?'

'No point in hangin' round here all mornin'.' He looked round at Stewart and the blood that was coming from the wound in his shoulder. 'Can you use this thing in your state?' he asked, nodding down at the Sharps.

'Reckon.'

'Okay, get up here an' cover me. I don't see them bein' up to much. If'n they sticks their heads out you know what to do.'

Stewart nodded, then grimaced. 'Sure. One thing, Jed.'

'Yep?'

'This bullet I took. It weren't no Double C. Came from upstairs in The Cattlemen's House. Faulkner.'

'You sure 'bout that?'

'Saw him after he backshot me. Plain as day.'

'Right.'

Herne passed Stewart the gun and waited until he'd got up to the edge of the building. The next moment he was sprinting across to the far side of the street, keeping his body low and firing as he ran. He didn't expect to hit anyone moving at that speed, simply keep them back. But Stewart did. Another of the Double C showed too much of himself trying to get a shot at Herne's running figure and the Sharps sent a bullet through his gun arm.

Herne skidded to a halt and rolled to his right, going for the cover of the nearest wall. But the sound of running feet told him that they weren't going to have any more to worry about from the Double C. Now that he'd shown up again, they'd seen the sense in getting out while they still could.

Which left Quentin Faulkner.

Herne waved a signal to Stewart and got to his feet, holstering his Colt and heading down the street. The folk outside The Cattlemen's House made way for him to pass between them.

The bodies of Miller and one of his men still lay untouched in the street, ignored except for a little girl in a pretty gingham dress who was bending over Scott Miller's huge, dead shape and wondering why he didn't answer her when she spoke to him. All she wanted was for him to get up and play.

Herne pushed open the doors and stood just inside the saloon. Bottles, glasses, all stopped on their way to open mouths; eyes turned to him and watched; no one spoke.

'Faulkner?' he asked.

Still nobody said anything. Then one of the girls in emerald green nodded in the direction of the office. When Herne started to head that way, she turned her back and pushed her way through to the centre of the horseshoe bar.

The door was locked and Herne took a step back and aimed a kick with the underneath of his boot at the wood alongside the lock. There was a loud splintering of wood and the door sprang open.

Herne went inside fast.

Faulkner was standing at the far side of his desk. There was a case open beside him and the contents of his safe were on the surface of the desk, but he hadn't put them inside the case. Possibly he hadn't had time; perhaps he'd seen fit to change his mind.

He was wearing the same blue suit Herne had first seen him in and the diamond tie pin was still in his cravat. What interested Herne most was the pistol he held in the podgy fingers of his right hand.

Not that the gun was threatening him: Faulkner was holding it against his own jaw.

Herne thought the man should be looking frightened, but he wasn't; his hand was steady and his eyes were clear. Herne thought maybe he knew why Faulkner hadn't gone through with packing the cash and papers from his safe.

He moved his mouth to speak: 'My affairs, Mister

Herne, seem to be in some disarray.'

Then he squeezed the trigger and blew half of his head off.

Dan Stewart lay propped up by a couple of pillows and the colour had more than come back to his cheeks. His shoulder was still heavily bandaged, but the doc reckoned it would get as good as new given rest.

Herne stood alongside the bed, looking down. He'd stayed around for a few days but now his things were packed up on his horse and he was ready to be away.

The big herds were due into Cheyenne and maybe after that he'd take a trip east. Omaha. See Long John and help him to ride his favourite horse one last time.

'Jed, I . . .'

Herne waved it away. 'I know. And it ain't worth talkin' about.'

Dan Stewart grinned. 'Thanks, Jed. Thanks a whole lot.'

He reached out his hand and Herne took it without hesitation and shook it firmly. Then, with a nod and a final word, he left the room and headed out to where his horse was waiting, impatient to be gone.

BORDEN CHANTRY
by LOUIS L'AMOUR

The marshal's name was Borden Chantry. Young, lean, rugged, he'd buried a few men in this two-bit cowtown—every single one killed in a fair fight. Then, one dark, grim day a mysterious gunman shot a man in cold blood. Five bloody murders later, Chantry was faced with the roughest assignment of his life—find that savage, trigger-happy, troubleshooter before he cut down every man in town . . . one by one . . .

0 522 10639 9—**65p**

TO THE FAR BLUE MOUNTAINS
by LOUIS L'AMOUR

For some men, an acre of land and a cottage are enough: not for Barnabas Sackett—the wanderlust in his blood drove him from the peaceful fen country of England over the sea to the New World. The call of the West was strong, and with Abigail beside him—and a Queen's warrant for his arrest behind him—Barnabas turned his face to the far blue mountains of Virginia. . . . He and his followers fought off wild beasts, shot buffalo and just about kept themselves alive—and at last they built their stockade on the James River. For a while, all was peaceful. Then one night, there were noises outside the stockade and, in a flare of torch-light, a dozen savage, painted faces . . .

0 522 10550 3—**65p**

SET A-FOOT
by J. T. EDSON

In the days of the open range, a cowhand's most vital possession was his horse. When a cowhand left a spread with no mount of his own, the rancher would usually allow him to borrow one from the remuda, but sometimes, if they parted on bad terms, this loan would not be made . . . There was no greater disgrace for a cowhand than to be set a-foot. It meant he was untrustworthy, and once the news got around, he would find it almost impossible to get another job. So when a cowhand was set a-foot, there was usually trouble—and often gun play.

Dusty Fog knew this, but he still set a-foot the man he blamed for the loss of an OD Connected trail herd and the injuries to some of the crew. He knew too that the cowhand he was disgracing was real fast with a gun—and knew that gun might be turned against him. The cowhand's only name was Waco . . .

0 552 10660 7—**65p**

OLE DEVIL AT SAN JACINTO
by J. T. EDSON

In 1835, the oppressions of Presidente Antonio Lopez de Santa Anna had driven the colonists in Texas to rebellion. Major General Sam Houston, realising that his small force could only hope to face the vast Mexican army when conditions were favourable, had ordered a tactical withdrawal to the east.

At last, on Thursday, April 21st, 1836, Houston decided that the time had come to make a stand. The Mexican Army, fifteen hundred strong, was on the banks of the San Jacinto river: Houston, with half that number, launched the attack that would decide the future of Texas.

0 552 10505 8—**60p**